The Beachcombers

Also published by Helen Cresswell and available from Hodder Children's Books

Bag of Bones
Snatchers
The Night-Watchmen

The Bagthorpe Saga
Ordinary Jack
Absolute Zero
Bagthorpes Unlimited
Bagthorpes v. the World
Bagthorpes Abroad
Bagthorpes Haunted
Bagthorpes Liberated

And for the younger readers:
The Little Sea Horse
The Sea Piper
The Little Grey Donkey
A Game of Catch
The Winklesea Trilogy

The Beachcombers

HELEN CRESSWELL

Hodder Children's Books

a division of Hodder Headline

First published in 1972 by Faber & Faber Limited

This edition published in 2000
by Hodder Children's Books
a division of Hodder Headline
338 Euston Road, London NW1 3BH

10 9 8 7 6 5 4 3 2 1

A Catalogue record for this book is available
from the British Library

ISBN 0 340 73657 7

Typeset by Avon Dataset Ltd, Bidford-on-Avon, Warks
Printed and bound in Great Britain by
The Guernsey Press Co. Ltd, Channel Isles

Hodder Children's Books
a division Hodder Headline
338 Euston Road
London NW1 3BH

www.headline.co.uk
www.hodderheadline.com

Dedicated to the memory of
Sidney Robbins
St. Luke's College, Exeter
1967–1971

Preface

It was Ned who wrote this story, of course. It could have been no one else. Only Ned could have known so much about the two worlds of the Dallakers and the Pickerings – so much *detail*, from the scarred and barnacled sides of the *Sea Queen*, to the stained oilcloth on that scullery table in the dark basement.

I wish I had known him – or knew him now, even, because for all anybody knows he is alive still – grown up now, of course, but still Ned for all that.

I advertised in *The Times* newspaper for three weeks running:

"Will the person known as Ned who sends

things to sea in bottles please contact Box BNR 360."

There was no reply – or not from Ned, at any rate. There were one or two letters from inquisitive people who wanted to know what the message meant, but that was all.

What the message meant is that I had picked up a large green glass bottle on the beach last year near Brancaster, on the Norfolk coast. I was looking for angels' wings at the time. The bottle was corked, and I thought I could make it into a reading lamp, perhaps, so I took it down to the sea and washed it. When I held it up to the light I saw the roll of paper, spiralling inside the thick green glass, making it seemed whorled, like a shell. I should think I felt much as Ned himself did when *he* found the bottle with a message. But what I found was a great deal more exciting and interesting than *his* find.

It was a thick bundle of fine quarto paper, handwritten so closely that it was nearly as difficult to decipher as Beatrix Potter's diaries. By the time I had read the first few pages I was determined to finish reading it if it took me the rest of my life. (It didn't. About a month, actually.)

When I had read it I spent another month

typing it out and then sent it to my publisher's editor. She and I both felt that it should be made into a book, but for one *enormous* snag. We sat up all one night discussing and arguing this way and that, and what we finally decided is obvious by the fact that you are at this moment reading this book.

What that snag was, you will find out later. Then you will be able to judge for yourselves whether or not we made the right decision.

Before you begin, imagine *yourself* down on a bare East Coast beach, searching for a pair of unchipped angel's wings. And imagine yourself finding among the tangled weed a large bottle of thick green glass, holding it up to the light, making out the faint whorls of the bundled papers inside. How you would run down to the sea's edge, as I did, and hold up the washed bottle again to the light. You were right! There *was* something!

Then the sharp crack of glass on stone, the green petals falling outwards on to the sand like a flower unfurling and there, in the centre, the thick bundle of handwritten papers, themselves uncurling slowly as if stretching after a long cramp. How you would stare, unable at first to believe what your own eyes were telling you, and then at last, deaf to the gulls and waves, blind to everything but that sheaf of papers, you would stretch out a trembling hand, pick them up, and begin reading . . .

Chapter 1

The three Pickerings sat and stared at him. Ned was reminded of Samuel Whiskers and tribe. It was something to do with pointed noses, sharp eyes, alertness. It was something to do with the room, which was a basement and had a smell of lino and turpentine and strong glue. It was a room that gave the impression of having been *scratched* together.

Ned faced the Pickerings, sitting side by side, and the bare light bulb dangled between them and he felt like an actor. He hesitated, because he was not sure what part they were expecting him to play. They had hurried down the stone steps, unlocked the door, almost scurried to their chairs, and now sat watching him. On one side his case stood beside him, on the other was a chair. Awkwardly he stepped sideways and sat on it.

Next minute he was on the floor, legs in the air, head in painful collision with something behind him. There was instant scuffle and confusion, sharp shrill cries, hands tugging at his coat. He looked up and saw their faces from a different angle, framed against the peeling plaster of the ceiling, and still he saw them sharp – sharper, even. From Mr Pickering's pocket a length of rope dangled – like a tail. Ned pulled himself up, confused.

"O fancy, to pick that!" cried Mrs Pickering. "To pick *that* one, eh, Jack? Eh, Arthur?"

"Not hurt?" enquired Mr Pickering, not quite meeting Ned's eye – almost, but not quite.

"I'm all right, thanks." He stepped back instinctively from Mrs Pickering's busy hands – brushing, tweaking, *pattering* over his coat. "Really."

"But to pick that one!" cried Mrs Pickering again. She pulled off her coat and threw it on another chair and Ned saw that there were at least a dozen chairs in the room – perhaps two dozen. He could hardly stand there counting them, but far more than the Pickerings would need – and not even a table to go with them.

"There's one or two shaky," said Mr Pickering. "Want glueing."

The smell of glue.

"But to pick one that *looks* as if it's four legs, but *ain't*!" cried Mrs Pickering. "You can *see* half the others is broke."

Ned took another look. So they were. Broken. Junk.

"You'll have to get glue, Arthur, glue, Jack, and get glueing. Though I do believe he picked it out o' purpose! I *do* believe he's going to turn out a rascal!"

She peered archly at Ned over her shoulder on her way to the peeling brown door in the far corner. She went out and Ned heard water spurting into a kettle or saucepan and saw that Mr Pickering and Jack were both looking at him as if for signs that he might turn out to be a rascal. Ned felt very unlike a rascal. What he felt was cold and tired and as bewildered as he had ever felt in his life before.

"Going to like it here?" asked Mr Pickering abruptly.

Ned had hardly been given time to decide. But he nodded.

"Jack'll watch you, Jack'll show you. *He* knows the ropes."

He took off his coat, a grease-stained mackintosh. Underneath he wore a suit tightly buttoned over a fraying grey pullover that hung below the edges of his jacket. Thin wrists poked from the too-short sleeves.

"Coat off?" he enquired.

Ned unfastened his own duffle and took it off, trying not to shiver.

"You come in here and have a cuppa tea," came Mrs Pickering's voice. "You come in the scullery to the warm."

The others obeyed, leaving Ned to follow. The smell in the scullery was of onions and – overpoweringly – paraffin.

"You get round the stove, you rascal," said Mrs Pickering. She wiped her hands on her overall and darted him another look that seemed to say that she, too, despite appearances, was a rascal, that they were conspirators.

"You'll like bloater paste and bakewell tarts?" she enquired.

Ned was blank.

"Not *together*, silly! Not spread *on*! D'ye hear that, Arthur? *You* fancy bloater paste on bakewells, do you? Eh – we *are* going to get on, you and me. Rascal, you!"

Ned, hunched over the fuming stove, tried again to seem rascally.

"If he ain't a rascal now," he heard Mr Pickering say in a low voice, "he will be!" and he saw Mr Pickering's elbow shoot out and dig into his wife's green overall, and heard her "Shush up, will you?" and saw Jack's pale face twist into a thin smirk, and wondered where on earth he had got to.

"Jack, you nip and fetch another chair," said his mother. "One with *legs*, eh? Oh dear! With legs!"

She gave the oilskin cloth a swift wipe and began to whisk out cups, saucers, plates with really astonishing speed and deftness. A coronation mug, chipped. Yellow cup, pink saucer – nothing matching. *Scratched* together.

Bakewell tarts in a cardboard box were produced from a string bag, followed by a jar of pink paste, a sliced loaf and a packet of margarine.

"I did a good shop," she said, catching his eye. "Give him a good tea off the train I said, didn't I, Arthur? He'll want a good tea."

Mr Pickering was lighting a cigarette and did not reply. He puffed several times in rapid succession as if trying to produce a smoke screen.

"Shan't be a tick," said Mrs Pickering. Ned could see that she would not. The knife flashed from marge to bloater and back to marge again.

"You go'n have a poke round." This to Ned.

"Poke round?"

"Show him, Jack. Get his case put in the room. And you show him that bunk Arthur's made him. You'll like that, won't you? You'll like to share with Jack – *what* tricks there'll be!"

She dug with her elbow but could not stop spreading so the dig went into thin air. Ned stared at Jack's thin, watchful face.

"I – I don't mind sleeping on my own," he said. "The advertisement–"

"Oh *that*! We thought it over, Arthur 'nd me, and knew you'd like to be in with Jack. And the other room's taken. There's a–"

She shot a glance towards her husband.

"Lodger," he prompted, appearing briefly from behind his smoke screen and immediately puffing up another. "Lodger, Mother."

"There's a Lodger coming," she said, buttering. "Not here yet, but coming. Isn't he, Jack, Arthur? Here in a day or two. Business gentleman – very quiet and respectable. Isn't he, Arthur?"

Jack jerked his head and made for the door and Ned followed. He picked up his case and went after him through the living-room, back past the stone steps and along a little dark passage.

"Ours." Jack stopped. He pointed at the other doors. "Theirs. His. W.C. Pull hard when you've finished."

"Oh, thanks," said Ned, and followed Jack into "ours". Jack pressed a switch and another naked bulb lit up. There was a small window, barred, high up on the opposite wall. Through a grey film Ned saw chipped bricks.

"Is the sea near?" he asked. He put down his case and noticed an old iron bedstead and another, lower one which he took to be the bunk.

"The what?"

"Sea."

"Oh. Nearish. What you got in there?" A jerk of the head towards the suitcase.

"Clothes. You know – toothpaste and things. A few books." Jack shrugged.

"C'mon."

Back in the scullery the Pickerings were already seated and the teapot was on the table.

"Pull up," said Mrs Pickering. She gave Jack's

hand a swift slap as he reached for a sandwich, then with the other hand began to pour the tea with swift, expert, swooping tilts, as if she knew the teapot's ins and outs, how to make it pour its best.

"Pass him a sandwich, Jack," she said sharply. "Mind your manners. And give your father one. And me." She took three sandwiches from the proffered plate and leaned back in her chair. It creaked loudly.

"Did you like the advertisement?" she asked. "Silly question – must've done, or you wouldn't be here, would you? It was me that wrote it. You wasn't the only reply we got, you know. Got five, didn't we, Arthur? But yours was the most – the most – suitable."

Ned said nothing. He felt suddenly unbearably sick – or homesick. He gulped, forcing down the bloater and margarine.

"Very sensible, your mother, we thought," continued Mrs Pickering. "We could tell from the letter. 'Kill two birds with one stone,' she says, more or less, 'Give him a break, and give me one.' Even offered to pay."

"Should've taken it," said Mr Pickering thickly.

She gave him a quick frown and shake of the head.

"Where there's money paid, there's questions asked. No money – no snooping. All square and above board – free hospitality and holiday by the sea."

" 'Kindly couple offer free holiday in seaside home to boy aged 9–11 as company for only child. Own room. Good food.' "

It was Jack, in a long, expressionless chant, plate empty again, eyeing the good food.

"Very good, Jack," said Mrs Pickering. "Off by heart. Have that last bloater, if he doesn't want it."

"No thanks," said Ned. It would have been too late anyway.

Mrs Pickering reached for a cardboard bakewell and creaked back again.

"Not really what I'd expected," she said, looking at Ned. "Is he you, Arthur?"

There was no reply.

"Course, you don't really *expect* anything," she continued. "Not from an advert. Can't. You have what you get. Have a bakewell, dear."

Ned shook his head.

"Not hungry," she said. "It'll be the motion of the train."

"I think I *could* do with some fresh air," said Ned, truthfully.

"That's it!" she cried. "The very idea, eh Arthur? Eh Jack? While you go out and do a bit of–" she broke off. "While Jack gives you a hand with that job you're on. Like to go down and see the sea, would you?"

"Yes please, Mrs Pickering."

"Mrs Pickering? You can't call me that! Want to call me auntie, do you?"

She patted his hand with her quick, light palm, and gave him another of her conspirator's looks.

"You shall call Mr Pickering uncle, and me auntie. Just one big happy family. We *are* going to get on, aren't we, dear?"

With an enormous effort Ned managed one last rascally look, and made for the door.

"But you don't know where the sea *is*!" came a shriek after him.

"I'll find it!" he shouted back. He picked up his duffle. "Don't worry, I'll find it!"

Chapter 2

The wind was icy. Ned put his hands in his pockets and one of them found a piece of cardboard and he remembered it was the postcard his mother had made him write before he left home, to let her know he had arrived safely. He kept it in his hand so that he would not forget to post it, because he knew one thing for certain. If he did forget, she would come straight over here, or even ring the police and *then* come. And if she did come, he knew equally certainly, he would not be allowed to stay. Because his mother liked things to be what she called "nice", and whatever else it might or might not be Number Eleven Bakers Road was not what his mother would call "nice".

It was not what Ned would call nice either, but his reasons were less easily defined. They were to do with pointed faces, cornering eyes, little patting hands, secret digs and looks.

He stood on the corner of Bakers Road at a crossroads and the wind whipped him forward to another crossroads. He turned left towards the shops, knowing that he was going seawards. The street was almost deserted and more than half the shops were shut, some shuttered under the shabby arcade that ran down the left side. He was a stranger to the town but recognised instinctively the kind of straight, open-ended road that runs to the sea and stops (though all roads run to the sea and stop). He kept his eyes ahead, scanning for the first edge of sea on the horizon. Then it was suddenly there, a clear line, and he broke into a run so that he could see the grey band widening visibly.

The road did end at the sea. He found himself at the top of a kind of rough pullover. On either hand stretched sand dunes, moaning faintly, long grass wind-flattened and shining. Ahead lay the North Sea.

Ned ran down the concrete slope to the suddenly soft, pulling sand. Lower down, the beach was ribbed by the tide and when he reached that part he was queerly light-footed again and as he raced he could feel the ridges under his soles. Ahead the breakers, ten feet high, rose magnificently, paused, then squandered themselves in spray. The wind was suddenly company, suddenly *with* him, boisterous and buffeting so that Ned found himself lashing out with his arms as if he were shadow-boxing. He took a skipping turn and walked backwards, leaning on the gale, looking back towards the town. It had gone. He saw only the dunes and here and there the glimpse of a wooden bungalow or roof of a caravan.

With another wheeling turn he veered right, towards a low shoulder of land that pushed out into the sea, blocking the view and forming a barrier to the bay. He could see a figure in the distance. He began to zig-zag, lost in the push of the wind and the deafening noise of it all – water and air in an enormous barrage of power. His eyes ran water, his ears sang.

It was a girl. She walked along the tide line higher up the beach where weed and driftwood lay stranded. She was trailing something behind her – a large, blackened net, as if she were trawling.

"Dry fishing," Ned thought, and broke into

another run, knees forcing the wind.

"Hey!" he shouted, and heard his voice fly straight past over his shoulder – almost as if someone else had spoken. "Hey!"

But the wind was whipping his voice away before it was even out of his mouth. And the girl, too, would be deafened. He saw her stoop and pick up a piece of wood, then drop it into the mouth of the net. She carried on. The net trailed flat behind her, scrawling the wet sand. Ned turned up the beach and began to follow. The marks had wiped out the girl's own footprints, making her seem oddly anonymous and out of reach.

But in a minute or so he drew level and she looked sideways at him. Because they were alone on the wide beach they looked at each other in a way they would never have looked if they had passed in the street.

"Hello."

"Hello."

"Collecting wood?"

He found that he was shouting – having to. He gestured towards the net – an old fishing net blackened by water and tar and patched with string (he remembered briefly the string bag and the Pickerings).

She nodded and stooped for a broken spar, worn smooth as a tooth.

"I'll help you find some." He looked about him and seized another piece lying by his feet. She held open the mouth of the net and he dropped it in. She began to walk on and he kept level with her.

"Is it for the fire?"

No reply.

"There's a big piece. Too big?"

"Father'll split it."

He ran and lifted one end.

"Too heavy."

"Not in the net. It'll pull easy enough."

Ned heaved the timber on to one end and she dragged the net right up, gathering up its neck, and dropped it over the top, hooding it.

"Like this, see. Now let go."

He gave the timber a push away from him and it fell squarely into the net and she gave it a neat, upward pull as the spar fell and it was bagged.

"I'll help pull."

She unclenched her mittened fingers and let out some rope. He took it and they breasted the wind together, plodding in step as if they were in harness.

"It's not so bad," he said. "Not so heavy as you'd think."

"The rope takes it."

"What's your name?"

"Fiony."

"Fiona, you mean?"

"Fiony," she repeated.

"Oh well, same thing, I expect. Just the way you say it."

She dropped her rope and walked off and stooped for a dried, whitish branch, like bone, curiously twisted.

"That's pretty," she said, half to herself, holding it at arm's length.

"Like a kind of skeleton."

"It is a skeleton. Of a tree."

"I suppose so. If you look at it like that."

She gave it a final look before dropping it into the net with the rest. They went on.

"D'you live near here?"

No reply.

"*I* don't. I'm just on holiday. If you could call it that."

She showed no sign of curiosity or interest. Piqued, he remembered that she had not even asked his name in return.

"My name's Ned. Ned Kerne. What's yours?"

"I told you."

"I meant your *other* name."

"Oh. Dallaker."

"Fiona Dallaker," he repeated.

"Fiony."

"Sorry – Fiony." He took a backward look over his shoulder and saw that the sky was darkening. "Are you going much further?"

"I'm going home," she said.

"Lucky you," he heard himself saying. Then, quickly, "Is it much further?"

"Why did you say that?" Now, at last, she was interested, he could sense her sideways look at his face.

"Say what?" he asked, knowing full well.

"About being lucky."

"Just a remark, that's all. *Is* it far?"

"See that?" She was pointing to the low headland, about half a mile off now. "The other side of there. You go off now, if you want. Father'll be waiting when I get there to pull the net over the dunes."

"I think I *had* better go," said Ned. "My friends will be expecting me."

"Thank you for helping." She shouldered the rope, ready to go.

"See you again, I expect."

He turned and faced the dark and let the wind carry him.

Chapter 3

"Dear Mother, I hope you are well and Duke as well. Mr and Mrs Pickering live about five minutes from the sea. I am sharing a room with Jack as Mrs Pickering has let the spare room to a lodger. He has not come yet but his name will be Mr Blagger. I have not had time to make many friends yet but I met a girl called Fiona Dallaker. Mr Pickering mends chairs and the cooking is not as good as at home but I am all right."

Ned re-read the letter and added the words "and enjoying myself" because he knew that at the very first sign of his seeming homesick or unhappy she would take the first train down – even if it meant her losing her job to do so.

She had wanted him to enjoy himself, have a holiday by the sea.

"Because you see, dear, there isn't enough money left for us to go to the sea this year, as we used to. Perhaps next year, if I save and save, we could take a little flat somewhere – go for a whole fortnight. And this is the most marvellous chance – the whole Easter holiday by the sea – and with a boy of your own age – you'll love it, Ned, and I shall too, thinking of you there by the sea. You *would* like to go, wouldn't you?"

He had felt a little ashamed at the time to admit that he would, without her. But he had remembered the Christmas holiday, spent cooped in the house or aimlessly wandering the neighbourhood, eating at other people's houses, waiting for six o'clock when his mother would come home tired out and pretending not to be. Besides, it had seemed like a real adventure to set off like that, by himself, to an unknown destination.

He *had* wanted to come here, and so it was partly pride that would not let him admit already that perhaps he had made a mistake. But it was also because he remembered how carefully his mother had prepared things ready for him to go – bought him new clothes, mended up his old ones. And then there had been the train fare to find.

"She said she'd try and come and see me one weekend," he reminded himself. He shut his eyes for a moment and saw a picture of their living-room at home with its cream-tiled fireplace with bookshelves either side, the pots of bulbs on the window-sill, Duke's basket by the hearth. Everything was still there, just as he had left it, and in less than a month's time he would be there again and the Pickerings nothing but a memory.

"I'll stick it out," he decided, writing the envelope. "It might not be so bad."

He pulled off his socks and changed into a pair of gymshoes ready for the beach. He would be going there alone again.

"Can't make it *out*," he thought. "The whole point of asking me was to keep Jack company. That's what I thought."

And Jack had gone off with his father the minute breakfast was over. Even the night before as they lay in bed in the darkness he had merely grunted in reply to Ned's whispered questions. In fact one of the things that had made getting to sleep so difficult for Ned himself was the sound of Jack's snoring.

Ned put the envelope in his pocket, picked up his plastic football and went back to the living-room. Mrs Pickering was in the scullery and seemed to be talking to herself.

"Is there anything I can do to help?" asked Ned, because his mother had told him to be sure to ask this as often as he could.

"Oh!" She turned from the sink. "I was just saying to myself – Mrs Pickering's got a cough, dear, and not feeling up to sorts."

"I'm very sorry. Perhaps you should go to bed?"

"Oh, I couldn't do that!" she cried. "If I was to go to bed every time I felt out of sorts, I should lose the use of my legs! No – it's the glue, dear. Gets on my chest. I was telling Mr Pickering only last night, 'It gets on my chest, Arthur, all this glue hanging about the place, and gums me up that I can hardly breathe. You'll have to think of another line, Arthur,' I says."

"But I thought that *was* Mr Pickering's line – mending chairs, I mean."

"Oh as to *lines*!" she cried. "Mr Pickering's got a thousand of 'em! Hasn't he, J–," she broke off. Jack was not there.

"What exactly does he do, then, Mrs Pickering?"

"He does what he can, dear, according to what's going," she replied.

"Oh!" Ned turned this remark over in his mind, certain that it *had* a meaning, if only he could see it.

"He's milked the chairs dry, that's what I tell him," she went on. "What with Easter coming on, and the spring cleaning, he should take advantage, and turn his hand to Miscellaneous."

"Miscellaneous?" repeated Ned, more mystified now than he had been before the conversation began.

"I like Miscellaneous, anyhow," she continued. "It's just like Christmas, sometimes, when he unloads the back of the van. And there's stuff I can keep, see. We've not had a Miscellaneous since we've been here, and I'm short on about everything you could mention – crocks, curtains, clothes. Oooh, I've had some lovely things – you'd be surprised. You can live like lords on the stuff they throw out!"

Ned thought that the kind of lords who lived like the Pickerings must be very eccentric, but thought, too, that he now had a glimmer of an idea what Mr Pickering's line of business was. He must be a kind of second-hand dealer – the phrase "rag and bone man" came into his mind but he pushed it firmly out again – mainly because he knew what his mother's reaction to *that* would be.

"I'll tell him when he comes in," she decided out loud. "It's just the right time of year – and Jack at home to lend him a hand. And you'll help with the sorting, won't you, dear?"

"Yes, of course."

"That's settled, then. He shall drop Chairs, and do some Knocking."

"On doors, you mean?"

"House to house Knocking. Arthur's a dab hand, despite he fights shy of it." She dropped her voice. "Thinks it's *lowering*. You might think all of it's lowering, eh, dear? You with your nice clothes – oh, I've seen what you've got in that case – and talking so nicely, too. Come from a good home, you do, we can see that. Quite a cut or two above what we'd expected, see?"

Ned stared at her, her dark little eyes intent on his own, her thin fingers tugging at her dangling belt. She seemed to be waiting for him to say something.

"No – really, Mrs Pickering," he stammered, feeling his face burn and really detesting her at that moment, with her embarrassing stare and head thrust forward. "I think it's very nice here, really I do. And I don't think it's lowering at all. I think it must be very interesting," he finished lamely.

"But you see, dear," she said, voice lower than ever now, "it's only in the *meantime*."

Ned, bewildered, stared back at her.

"It's all," she waved her hands about her at the dark scullery, "in the meantime. All of it. The day's to come, and soon to come," she smiled, but Ned did not like the smile, or return it, "when we shall be up, up, up in the world like shooting stars! No more Knocking, no more Chairs or Tables or Miscellaneous! Up, up, *up*!"

Both arms shot up and she stood momentarily stiffened like a character in a play before the curtain drops.

Ned, too, felt stiffened into his stare. Whatever was he meant to say, what part was *he* supposed to act? Abruptly her arms dropped, her shoulders rounded and she was her wheedling self again.

"You'd like to see us go up in the world, wouldn't you, dear?" she said.

"Of – of course."

"And I daresay you'd help us, if you could?" She came nearer, hands twitching. In another minute she was going to pat him again.

"Of course I would, Mrs Pickering!" he cried, and stepped back.

"Auntie. Like to call me auntie, wouldn't you? Just like one of the family."

"All right! Auntie!" He had backed right out of the scullery now and stumbled against one of the chairs and for a moment was seized by a desperate impulse to run – right out of the house, right away from Eleven Bakers Road and the dirty, inexplicable Pickerings into the safe, sane, ordinary world outside.

The chair had fallen with a clatter and Ned picked it up and put himself on the far side so that the chair was between him and Mrs Pickering's hands.

"I'll help, Mrs Pick – Auntie – I'll help, really I will," he said. "I could go Knocking, if you like. I might not be very good at it, but I'll try. And I'll help sort. I'll–"

"Bless us!" Her hands flew up again. "*That* ain't what we're after! You're a nice boy, you are, and Knocking's lowering – your ma wouldn't want you Knocking, would she?"

"I – I don't know, Mrs – Auntie."

"Nothing at all like that, dear. Come for a holiday, you have, and build you up nice and strong by the sea. *Ever* such a little thing it is you can do to help us. And if it all comes off, you and your ma'll come up in the world too, and you'd like that, wouldn't you, dear? Like to help your dear mother, would you?"

"Yes. Yes – of course!"

"*Course* you would. There's not a lad in the world wouldn't want to – look at our Jack. *Nothing* he wouldn't do for me."

"What would you like me to do, then?"

"Only listen to him!" cried Mrs Pickering. "Can't hardly wait to get started, bless his heart! There's nothing *now*, dear. You get off down the sea and enjoy yourself. Mr Pickering and me'll give the word, when we're ready. But I'm glad we had this little talk. I shall tell Mr Pickering the minute he gets back, and he'll be that delighted he'll give you ten pence, I shouldn't wonder."

"There's no need for him to do that!" Ned cried. "So I'll go now, shall I? And be back at dinner?"

He turned and as he did so felt a hand at his sleeve.

"I spy!" cried Mrs Pickering. "What do I spy?"

Swift as lightning a hand flew out and whisked back again – holding an envelope.

"There! I knew it! A real mother's boy! Written

a letter to his ma already, and not a day gone since he left home. Told her all that's happened, have you, and what a good time you're having?"

"Yes, I – I was just telling her how nice it was and – I was just going to get a stamp for it." He put out his hand for the letter.

She snatched it back, merry and coy.

"Ooops! *Nearly* got it! Going to spend your money on a stamp? You get off and buy yourself an ice-cream. Auntie'll post it when she goes to shop. I know boys – in your pocket all day it'll be, if I know what rascals boys are – kicking their footballs and running about and never a thought of their dear mothers waiting for news of them. *Off* you go now, dear!"

Ned hesitated, torn between the desire to get away and reluctance to leave his letter in those busy, restless fingers.

"*Off* you go!"

Her playfulness was fading now. In another minute it would have vanished entirely, and who knew then what her mood would be? Ned did not wait to find out. He fled.

Chapter 4

He was only a few yards away now from the headland and a new view. As he climbed the dunes the soft sand slithered under his feet so that each step forward was also half a step backward. He grasped at the tufts of coarse grass to pull himself up, finding the slope longer and steeper than he had thought it. Even when he seemed to have reached the top all he could see ahead were more dips and hillocks, and when the view did come it was suddenly.

Like all the best views it was unexpected, so unlike what he had imagined that he stopped dead in his tracks to take it in. What he had imagined was another miles-long stretch of sand like the one behind him, the kind of beach he had always been used to on holidays spent along the East Coast. What he saw was a small, half-moon bay sheltered on three sides by high dunes. The tide was low, leaving exposed a wide band of mud flats.

High and dry up the beach was a large boat, flat-bottomed and sturdy yet half-magical too in its sheer unexpectedness under the bleak East Coast light. Its three tall masts and slender cross-spars were finely etched against the near white sky. The waterline showed dark on the barnacled sides. The boat was real. It was impossible yet anchored – truly anchored with a great rusted chain trailing from the side.

White gulls carelessly walked the decks and festooned the spars like buntings, the only sign of life, except – Ned's heart jumped. Smoke was rising, in a thin blue line – he sniffed – wood smoke. Then, higher up the beach at the foot of the dunes, he noticed a great pile of driftwood heaped like a bonfire as if the occupants of the boat were marooned and waiting to signal a passing boat.

Driftwood. Logs and spars trawled in a net. Fiony. "I live just over the dunes."

A man appeared on deck. He was very tall

and thin, spidery among the rigging, dressed in loose seaman's blue. He swiftly scanned about as if from old habit, and saw Ned. An arm was raised in greeting.

"Ahoy!" he shouted.

Ned hesitated. Then, with a rush of excitement, an almost unbearable sense of adventure in the offing, he lifted his own arm.

"Ahoy!" he yelled, and made down the steep bank, slithering and stumbling in his haste. About thirty yards off he paused. The man was still there, watching him with a half-smile.

"Does Fiony Dallaker live here?"

"You the lad that helped her with the wood?"

"Yes, I met her yesterday. I'm Ned Kerne."

"Fiony's father. Dallaker's the name."

"How do you do, Mr Dallaker," said Ned. He was right by the boat now, close enough to touch the crust of barnacles – which he did – and tilted back his head to look up at Mr Dallaker's boots and beard, mainly.

"Come aboard," invited Mr Dallaker.

"Oh *may* I? Thanks!" He looked about him, then ran up to the bow, mystified.

"How?" he called.

"Round to starboard."

Ned went right round the bows, and craning

up could make out the name *Sea Queen* carved on the side.

"Oh!" He stopped short. Only a few yards away, seated on upturned crates, were Fiony and a grizzled old man wearing a peaked cap.

"Hello!" he cried, greeting her like a long-lost friend (and she *was* the nearest thing he had to a friend in this place). She looked startled, but smiled back.

"I was just looking for the way up," he explained.

She pointed, lifting a wet hand from a bowl of water in which she was peeling potatoes. Ned saw a thick rope ladder dangling over the side near the stern.

"Oh, thanks."

"You're welcome."

"And good morning," said the old man sternly. "Good morning, young feller." He turned to Fiony. "Good *morning*," he said meaningly.

"All right." She shrugged. "Good morning."

"It don't matter how far you live off civilisation," said the old man, "you keep your manners. I've been on islands and said good morning to savages, in my time."

"Yes, Grandad. But that was then – about five hundred years ago. *I* don't get said good morning to when I go up the town."

"What we was talking about," returned the other, yanking up a length of net and paying it out over his knee, "was what you say to *folks*, not what folks say to you."

"Yes, Grandad."

"And I don't have the pleasure of this young feller's name."

She got to her feet, hands and arms dripping.

"Mister Ned Kerne," she gestured airily – and wetly.

"Mister Dallaker Senior. The Captain."

"I'm very pleased to meet you," Ned said. "I met your granddaughter – she is, isn't she? – on the beach yesterday, and I saw your son – *is* he your son? – just now, the other Mr Dallaker, and he said I could come aboard."

"I am and he is," said Fiony. "In fact, both are."

"We're all Dallakers here," said the Captain.

"And have you just sailed in?" asked Ned. "Or do you live here? All the time, I mean?"

To him, both seemed equally impossible.

The Captain was slowly shaking his head and had begun paying the blackened net over his knee again. It dawned on Ned that he was not going to answer the question, and something in his sorrowful air suggested that the question had been lacking in manners in the first place.

"Is that lad coming aboard or isn't he?" called Mr Dallaker.

"Coming!" Ned ran and grasped the rope, wet and coarse. He could smell the salt and pitch in it. His eyes drew level with the deck and as he pulled himself over a pair of gulls fluttered noisily past his head and he looked back and saw the whipped sand below and was as good as at sea. And the sea itself looked different from up here, from behind masts and ropes and spars.

"Oh crikey," he said. "It's marvellous."

He knew nothing about boats and was dizzy with the suddenness of finding himself on the deck of this strange, stranded vessel, tackled and sea-stained and old as the hills and pointing her bows even now towards the sea. He stared about him, seized by the certainty that the worn, dry boards under his feet had been many times awash on the high seas, and by despair that he had not been there.

"Like her?"

"*Like* her?" Ned echoed. "She's fantastic. She's marvellous. *Sea Queen.* That's her name, isn't it?"

Mr Dallaker nodded.

"She's marvellous," repeated Ned. "I've hardly

been on any ships, Mr Dallaker. I'm a landlubber. But I bet there isn't another like her in the whole of England – in the world, even. When I saw her, I thought I was dreaming."

Mr Dallaker laughed outright.

"Did you, now! Taken a real liking to her, ain't you?"

"And I wonder *why*." Ned spoke softly, more to himself than anyone else. "I absolutely can't get over it. Her, I mean. I get a feeling – a feeling that she's been just about everywhere there is to go in the whole world, and seen just about everything there is to see. How old *is* she, Mr Dallaker?"

"Not of my day, and not of *his*" – a jerk of the head over the starboard side. "But a Dallaker, right enough. And as to her being everywhere – there's shot in her sides to prove it, and foreign words carved on her panels below. *We* know she's been everywhere. And you, young feller, you've come straight aboard this here ship and set your finger straight on the heart of the matter."

"Have I?" said Ned, surprised.

"Almost as if you'd knowed," said Mr Dallaker musingly.

"Known what, Mr Dallaker?"

"About the log." There was a silence. Ned waited for a clue. None came. In the end, Ned was forced to reveal that he had *not* known.

"Which log, Mr Dallaker?"

"Ship's log – *Sea Queen*'s – that goes back to the very beginnings. The ones that tell of how the shot got in her sides and the carvings below. Right to her beginnings. Think – the very day she first had her bottom wet, the day she first rolled a wave and had her sails set to the wind. And right to the beginnings of the Dallakers, too – two hundred years, three hundreds – thousands, even, we think sometimes. The old man" – another jerk of the head to starboard – "thinks of nothing else day and night. Keeps saying if only we had the log safe he could die easy."

"But he's not going to die, is he?" cried Ned, alarmed.

"In the end. We all are. Ten years for him maybe – God willing and accidents preventing. It's the Cap'n's way of speaking, you understand. I might say the same thing myself. I could go to my rest with the log back in its rightful place. We *all* could."

If the whole Dallaker family was likely to go to their rests the minute the *Sea Queen*'s log was found, it seemed to Ned that it was well lost.

"But how did it get lost?" he asked. "And when?"

"1897. September 18th. Off the Dogger. In a storm."

"Well, that's it, then, isn't it?" cried Ned, half-relieved. "If it went overboard, that's it, isn't it? Even if you'd fished it straight out again, it'd have been ruined."

"I wasn't there," Mr Dallaker reminded him.

"Oh – no – of course not."

"And if I *had've* been, I should have plunged directly after it. Tempest or no tempest."

"Yes, I bet you would, Mr Dallaker," said Ned. "But it *is* too late, isn't it? I think it's a terrible shame and I'm really sorry you lost it, but it *has* gone, hasn't it?"

Mr Dallaker appeared to give the matter thought.

"Gone," he agreed at last, "but in good hands."

"Good hands?"

"The sea," replied Mr Dallaker. "None better. That log, young feller, was in four brass-bound books, see? And them four brass-bound books was in a brass-bound box."

"So it would float!"

"And that brass-bound box," said Mr Dallaker,

"has been a-floating ever since. We don't know where, but we guess. We guess in the North Sea, between the Dogger and the east coast of England."

"In fact it could be washed up here at any moment!"

"Oh young feller," said Mr Dallaker, "I take my hat off to you. You put your finger on things in a most marvellous way. And because you're a lad I like the looks of, a lad that's got eyes in his head to see straight off that the *Queen* is the finest timber that ever sailed the high seas, I shall let you into a secret. The Dallakers," he paused dramatically, "is here on a treasure hunt!"

Ned stared.

"I'm off now, Father," came Fiony's voice from below. "Just going up the town. Mother needs glue."

Glue. Ned's mind swung like a pendulum. Pickering Dallaker Pickering Dallaker tick tock tick tock . . .

"Will you come, Ned?" she called.

He climbed back down the rope ladder, slowly, searching the barnacles for scars and scorch marks.

"High tide at three, remember," called Mr Dallaker.

Ned looked back up at him, arms crossed and legs astride against the pearly sky and cross-spars.

"I'll come back and help, shall I?" he asked.

"That," said Mr Dallaker, "would be fully pleasant."

Once over the ridge of dunes the wind took hold of them again and they started to run, Fiony trailing the net.

"Aren't you looking for wood?" Ned called into the wind.

"Father and me reaped the night tide."

"In the middle of the *night*?" He pictured the beach at night and the two figures stooping, gathering, stooping, gathering.

"Dawn," she answered. "Dawn'll do, as long as we're first."

"I think it must be marvellous to get up and go along the beach at dawn," he said, picturing that, too.

"Oh it is – in summer. Trouble is, it's winter, half the year."

"Do you go collecting – I mean reaping – every tide?"

He swerved closer so that he could catch her answer whole, instead of only words, teasing clues and fragments tossed by the wind.

"Race you!" she shouted suddenly, and broke into a run again with Ned hard on her heels. He stamped his foot on the trailing net so that it jerked out of her hand and flew up as if it were alive. He tripped and stumbled to his knees and shrieking she ran back to retrieve the net and was ahead of him again. The sun came out and the shadows wheeled over the beach in wide bands and Ned tried to race that, too, but in the end could catch neither Fiony nor the sun and gave up, panting.

When they neared the pullover Fiony dropped the net and collapsed beside it. She lay back with her arms crossed behind her head and closed her eyes. Driftwood. Wordlessly Ned sat beside her. After a while she got up and pulled the net up into the dunes to hide it.

Then they strode up the pullover and the town came into view and Fiony said absently:

"Glue. Musn't forget the glue."

Glue. The Pickerings. Ned set foot on land again and the Pickerings were only round the corner now. Fiony pulled a bag from her pocket and a piece of paper.

"Goodbye," she said, and was already pushing open the door of a shop.

"See you after dinner," Ned called after her and the door shut.

At Number Eleven Bakers Road Ned found the front door shut and locked. There were three bells with little cards beside each and he pressed the one labelled A Pickering and heard the bell ringing below. The rest of the house, he knew, was empty. Holiday flats. Between the iron railings he could see a light in the scullery window. He waited.

From over his shoulder a hand appeared. A thick, square-tipped finger pressed again on the bell for what seemed a very long time.

"Blagger," a voice said. "Name of Blagger."

The hand that had pressed the bell fell heavily on Ned's shoulder, and the door opened.

Chapter 5

The *Sea Queen* was afloat. Ned stared. He had not thought of that – riding at anchor at high tide, beached again at low. He walked along the tide line and stopped opposite her. Although she was close in, within hailing distance still, she seemed oddly remote and unattainable. She was in a different element now – her own element.

Ned, to whom the sea had always meant the place where the land ended, saw it now for the first time as something else, something in its own right. The Dallakers were afloat more than they were ashore – the water was their home too. And the life they led was infinitely trickier, more dangerous, than that of a landsman. You did not have to *learn* the land as you did the sea. The moods of the land were to do only with sun and shadow, weather and season – tame and plotted and easily dealt with. They could not force you into corners, cast you away on deserted islands, pick you up and smash you. They could not make you afraid.

He shivered briefly. Even the air seemed suddenly colder, more salt-laden and sea-smelling. The Dallakers, for all their easiness, were a race apart, and he a landlubber. He would never know them. To know them he would have to join them, and that was impossible.

The *Sea Queen* creaked as she swung at her moorings, see-sawed with the tide. Then Ned saw that near her stern where before the rope ladder had hung, a rowing boat and a dinghy were lying together alongside. The Dallakers were aboard.

He cupped his hands to his mouth.

"Ahoy!" he shouted.

"Ahoy!" Mr Dallaker had appeared almost instantly as if he had been sitting somewhere on deck all the time, merely waiting Ned's call.

Net watched him drop the ladder and climb down into the rowing boat. From there he scrambled over into the dinghy, and cast off.

With only a few swift, expert pulls he was ashore, wading the last few yards, towing the dinghy behind him. He pulled it up the beach, well beyond the tide line and its harvest of shells and weeds.

"I've come to help." Ned went to join him. "Isn't Fiony coming?"

"Asleep. They all are. There's a net here for you." He pulled out of the bottom of the dinghy what looked like an endless ravel of black string, and with a couple of tugs separated it, miraculously, into two nets.

"I'll take the town stretch," he said, "and if you're willing, you take yonder."

He nodded towards the far side of the bay, towards the headland.

"And what shall I look for?" Ned asked, keeping his own voice casual because Mr Dallaker himself seemed to take it so much for granted, as if he did it every day, setting on part-time beachcombers.

"Flotsam," Mr Dallaker told him, "and jetsam."

"Does that include wood?"

"It includes everything. Any sorting that's to be done, it'll be done when we get back to the *Sea Queen*. By a professional Beachcomber."

"Yes, Mr Dallaker," said Ned humbly.

"You keep your eyes skinned, and there's nothing you mightn't find! The tides is running up now for the spring, you can feel 'em tug. You've yet to learn, young feller, what a wave can bring. Just you rest easy, keep your eyes open and the net ready. The sea'll do all the work. Never been beachcombing before, I daresay?"

"I've walked *along* beaches," Ned told him. "Everyone has. And I've found things, too. I found a toy yacht, one year – nearly brand new it was. And I found a big rusty iron ball only Mother said I wasn't to touch it, said it could have been a mine."

"It was *proper* beachcombing I was referring to," said Mr Dallaker. "Beachcombing with *intent.* And I should advise you myself not to go meddling with any rusty iron balls. But all else, you just put it in the net, will you, and bring it back here."

"Oh I will," said Ned. "Absolutely everything."

He picked up the net and the coarse, tarry feel of it made him feel instantly a real beachcomber and glad that he was to go out alone – entrusted with a whole mile of tide line along the beach he had not yet even seen – the one that lay beyond the Dallakers' bay.

"You going to be all right?" asked Mr Dallaker, shouldering his own net with an easy swing. "I'm not to wake her?"

"No, don't wake her," said Ned quickly. "Please. I'll be quite all right, really."

He wanted to be a beachcomber alone. Besides, his friendship with Fiony would ripen the sooner if she was let sleep when she wanted to sleep. When she awoke and found her combing done by Ned, she would be grateful – more inclined to share secrets. And secrets they had, of that Ned felt certain.

He climbed the dunes and looked back for a last glimpse of the *Sea Queen*. She lay so comfortably in the mid-afternoon sun that it seemed to Ned that you could tell just by looking that everyone on board was asleep. Even the gulls were slumped and fat on rail and spar – fish-full, and napping. Ned caught a glimpse of Mr Dallaker's shoulders and head on the skyline but next minute they were gone. Ned set his own face towards the south and let the wind give him a last nudge towards yet another view.

He saw before him an endless beach and immediately wondered how he would tell a mile.

"I could walk halfway down the edge of

England," he thought, "if I didn't remember to turn round."

He scanned the frieze of dunes for landmarks but could see none. He glanced at his watch.

"I'll walk for half an hour," he thought, "or until the net's full, or until it rains. Whichever's first."

He started to walk, planting his feet firmly, walking with *intent*. He felt as if he had never properly been on a beach before. He went down, as Mr Dallaker had told him, to the tide line – newly damp and with a strong, fresh seaweed smell. The sea itself rose and dashed only a few feet away.

"A good beachcomber's always in wetting distance of the sea," Mr Dallaker had said earlier. Ned remembered his words now, spray cold on cheek and hands.

"I'm like an explorer," he thought. "No one's ever set foot here before. In a *way* they haven't."

The sea was wiping the sand clean as if it were a slate. It would be left printless, but newly and excitingly furnished with different shells, weed, starfish, driftwood – treasure.

Ned, not wishing to seem prying, had not asked Mr Dallaker again about the treasure, but he felt sure that he would recognize it at once if he should find it.

"And what if I were the one to find the brass-bound box!"

The thought was so unbearably exciting that he broke into a run, pulling up short a few yards on at the memory of yet another of Mr Dallaker's dictums:

"Slow and easy does it. You're *combing*, remember. Thorough."

Ned, mindful of the art of beachcombing, walked slowly again – with intent. By the time he had heaved a dozen or so timbers into the net and could feel it dragging, furrowing a trail, he could not have run even if he had tried.

Gathering timber was satisfying enough for a time, but when he glanced again at his watch and saw that the half-hour was nearly up, he began to feel misgivings. Surely there was more to beachcombing than this? "Flotsam and jetsam" Mr Dallaker had said. Was he missing something? And what *were* flotsam and jetsam? They conjured up visions of things rare and strange – frankincense and myrrh, Quinquireme of Nineveh . . .

He stopped and looked about him, vainly scanning the empty beach for signs of a miraculous haul spread for the taking. He saw purple weed and shining wet stones and splintered wood and – he stiffened. Ahead, right on the tide line, lay something that glittered. It glittered green – bottle-glass green.

Ned hauled furiously at the net, and as he drew nearer dropped the rope, all patience gone, and ran, rules forgotten.

It *was* a bottle. Ned stared at it first, lying bedded in a mass of weed of brighter green. It was a corked bottle. Gingerly he picked it up, fingers stiff and wary. Its lightness took him by surprise.

"It's empty!" he said out loud. In his disgust he almost flung it from him, but remembered in time the broken glass and thought, too, of something else. He held it up – not to the sun, because the sun had gone again – but against the part of the sky where the sun should be.

"Oh crikey!" he said. "There is! A message!"

Better than treasure, this, better even than a brass-bound box – in the way that any mystery is better than a plain fact.

He peered into the greenish glooms of the bottle, its magical depths, filled with curving lights and shades that could only be formed by a rolled-up paper – still caught in the long, thin neck, but fanning out at the bottom to touch the sides. It was a message – and the sea the messenger. But he could stand there till doomsday with the bottle corked and be none the wiser what its secret was. Clutching it tightly he let out a whoop and turned and raced back to where the net lay sprawled.

Halfway back towards the dunes he began to wish he had not been so thorough in his combing, and was tempted to stop and jettison part of his catch. (Perhaps *that* was where "jetsam" came from – it *sounded* nearly the same.) But it was his first time out as a beachcomber proper and too soon to begin breaking the rules. He was so hot that he took off his anorak, pushed the bottle carefully up one of the sleeves and placed the bundle in the mouth of the net. After that, pulling was easier.

When at last he reached the dunes he found why Fiony had needed her father's help the day before. The load that had travelled quite easily over the smooth sand, stamped firm by the tide, became suddenly twice its weight, and awkward, digging itself into the soft sand. With a struggle he managed to pull it behind the first mound, where it would be partly concealed. There he bent, gasping, to retrieve his anorak, and then ran.

Once over the brow of the dunes he could see the *Sea Queen* and the Dallakers – all ashore now. They were standing in a little knot and he could hear their excited voices, blown into fragments, as usual, by the wind.

"Ahoy!" he shouted, and brandished the bottle.

They whirled round.

"Ahoy!" he shouted again.

Fiony waved and he heard the Captain's voice in answer. He noticed as he scrambled down the last dune that Mr Dallaker was missing but that someone new was there – a lady, with long dark hair – Mrs Dallaker? He noticed, too, that they were very excited about something, and felt momentarily cheated. What had happened. Surely not the brass-bound box? Was his bottle going to fall flat? He tucked it under his arm and marched up to the group.

"Hello!" he said. (It sounded better than "ahoy!", close to.) "Is something the matter?"

"Oh, Ned!" cried Fiony. "It wasn't you, was it? You aren't playing tricks on us?"

"Tricks?"

"We've been napping," explained the Captain enigmatically, "and *caught* napping."

"How?"

In reply the Captain pointed.

"That," he said. "While we was napping."

He was pointing to the sloping stretch of sand left newly firm and wet by the ebbing tide. There was writing on it – enormous capitals scrawled in the sand by a stick or stone – scribbled fiercely by a heavy hand. The letters were all sideways on, so Ned edged round to the seaward side. There were just two words:

GO AWAY

"But who did it?" he asked stupidly. "Who would do that?"

"We don't know," replied the Captain. "But we guess."

"Who do you guess, then?"

He shook his head.

"It's a family business," he said. "Ain't it, Nell?"

Nell, who was the long-haired lady, nodded.

"The best thing," she said, "is wait for Matthew." She smiled at Ned then, a smile of singular sweetness – the best he had had since he left home.

Ned could contain himself no longer.

"I found this!" he blurted, and held up the bottle. "Right on the tide line. And it's still corked and there's some paper in it, a message, but I couldn't get it open so I brought it back here and can we *open* it, please? Please, quickly?"

The Dallakers gazed at the green bottle and Ned saw with triumph that the message was forgotten, that he held the stage. He saw them suddenly in tableau, all thin and all ragged, being played on by the wind.

The Captain stretched out a hand, and Ned passed over the bottle. The Captain held it up to the light just as Ned himself had done, squinting in a manner so pronounced and seamanlike that it seemed almost possible that he might be reading the message right through the glass. He then lowered the bottle and examined the cork with an expert eye.

"*This* ain't been long in the water," he observed. "Wetted, that's all."

"Perhaps someone's been shipwrecked!" cried Ned hopefully. "It could be someone shipwrecked and wanting help. *Please* open it, Captain Dallaker!"

The words were hardly out of his mouth when the Captain bent and an arm swung suddenly up and then down again. There was a sharp crack of glass on stone and the fragments fell outwards in a neat circle – as if a green flower had suddenly unfurled. In the Captain's hand was the bottleneck itself, and protruding from it the paper, changed in the twinkling of an eye from a mere greenish shadow to a bright, white reality in the shadowless coast light.

Ned gulped. He had hardly been able to wait for the bottle to be opened, but now that the paper was there, still rolled and secret, he could hardly bear for it to be opened and read. He met the Captain's bleached blue eyes.

"Your catch. You read it, young feller."

Ned gulped again and shook his head.

"*I* will!" Fiony stretched out her hand.

"All right!" Ned cried. "Give it me!"

The glass was warm now. Slowly Ned pulled the paper from the tight neck and it unfurled of its own accord. He straightened it, using both hands. The others watched.

"Come on!" Fiony cried. "What does it say?"

He looked up.

"It says GET OUT," he said.

Chapter 6

"Addressed to us," said the Captain at length, when the piece of paper had been passed round, stared at, turned over and upside down, and still could be made to say nothing either more or less than it seemed to say. The message was clear. GET OUT.

"But how can it be meant for us?" Fiony's face was white. "It came by sea. Anyone could've picked it up."

"Anyone?" put in her mother tartly. "With Dallakers in the offing?"

"I suppose not," she admitted.

"But how could the person who threw it have known it'd be washed up on this beach?" cried Ned. "It could've been washed up anywhere in the whole of England – or Scotland, even, or Ireland!"

"There's two things possible," replied the Captain thoughtfully. "Either it was thrown by an *expert* – meaning You Know Who – or else it wasn't thrown at all." He paused. "By the same person or persons," he added, as an afterthought.

It seemed to Ned that the Dallakers dealt in riddles as they dealt in driftwood. The Captain's last remarks might as well have been in Chinese for all the sense he could make of them.

"What you mean," said Fiony, "is that someone crept down the beach, and *put* the bottle there?"

"That," said the Captain, "is what I mean exact. Sharp lass. And what is furthermore, that same person or persons then came creeping up and writ this" – he waved a thin, booted leg – "in the sand."

"But the tide had only just turned!" cried Ned. "I'd have seen them, wouldn't I? They'd have to have been quick!"

"The persons *I'm* thinking of," returned the Captain, "*is* quick."

"Oh!" Ned glanced over the Captain's thin, stooping shoulders to the dunes beyond and wondered whether those same persons were there even now, at this very moment, watching.

"Here's Matthew now," said Mrs Dallaker. They heard his hail, saw his lank, striding figure. "Oh dear, how I wish we could sail right out of it all!"

"But you won't, will you?" Ned was alarmed.

"Oh no. We shan't. You can trust the Dallakers for that. If you was to trace 'em back far enough, you'd find a limpet somewhere at the beginnings. *Obstinate*...?"

"It's a matter of honour," said the Captain.

"And treasure," added Fiony.

Then Mr Dallaker was there and the explanations began. He listened, and he shook his head, and he looked at the messages, and he frowned. At the end, it all stopped abruptly, and Ned could hear again the hiss of the draining tide. He heard the long line of waves fall and crash before Mr Dallaker spoke.

"There's only one thing possible," he said at last. "Scavengers."

Another wave rose and fell.

"Living by the sea," Ned thought, "time is in waves, not in minutes."

"But – but they don't know where we are, Father!" Fiony's face was white again.

"We don't know where *they* are," he corrected.

"Different thing. They're quick and they're sly – *we* know that. They go into holes, underground. And we're washed up here square for the whole world to see if they've a mind to look. Wide open on a beach, aboard ship. That's the nub of the matter. They see us, we don't see them."

"But they've given up beachcombing! That's what you told us! Given up beachcombing, and turned inland scavengers."

"And why?" asked Mr Dallaker grimly. "And why? Because they were tired of being forever poor, they said. Because the riches of the sea wasn't enough for them. But what if" – he paused and let a wave fall – "what if they was to get wind of – treasure?"

Now in the silence that followed the very sand seemed to tick, Ned could hear the tiny bubbles bursting on sponge and weed, the whole beach in a soft explosion.

"And there's treasure coming." The Captain's voice was low now. "There's treasure on the spring tides. I've studied my almanacks and I've read the moon. But most I've dreamed, and they're queer things the sea'll give you if you listen while you sleep. I'm an old man now, with a head full of driftwood. Things float by now so I can't catch 'em. And I forget what time it is when I'm waking, and my hands slip when I tie knots, and every year the sounds and the voices get further and further away. But my dreams, they come greener than ever in the night, straight out of the sea into my old head, and *them* I hear. And it ain't the almanacks any more, it's neither the moons nor tides that tell me what I know now. It's the dreams."

The Captain jerked his head and they moved off and left him. The *Sea Queen* was almost aground now, and they waded to the rope ladder.

Once more on deck Ned felt again the age and mystery. The Dallakers themselves were like no one he had ever met before, and he thought that it must be something to do with living and working on this old ship. He wondered whether he, too, would be different if he lived here – undergo a kind of sea change.

"He's an old man," Mrs Dallaker said. She looked back over the rails to where the Captain sat now with his head drooping on to his chest, pouched like a bird.

"He really believes in it, doesn't he?" said Ned. "About finding the log."

"We all do," said Mr Dallaker. "Keeps life going forward. Every tide that comes up could be the one we're waiting for. I've reaped tides all my life, twice a day and three hundred and sixty-five days a year – or as many shore days as there's been in a year. And mostly it's been wood I've found – and grateful for it, don't mistake me. But I've found the wood looking for treasure, if you see what I mean. And to have a tide like that – once in a lifetime – well, it's what beachcombing's about, in a way."

"So if you do find the treasure, you'll give up beachcombing?"

"What?" He looked startled.

"I mean, if it only comes once in a lifetime, and you've *had* that once, there's not much point going on."

"When you've had it once," replied Mr Dallaker, "you start all over again. You *always* comb in the hopes of treasure."

"Shall you come below?" invited Mrs Dallaker. "I could give you some cake."

She led the way and Ned followed, heart beating furiously. He was to go below decks, into the inmost heart of the ship. The steps were steep and narrow – little more than a ladder – and they had to be descended backwards. Ned saw that the rungs he was holding were worn in the middle, scooped into arcs by the feet of generations of Dallakers.

"Here's the saloon," said Mrs Dallaker, and waved an arm. "I'll go finish the cake. Needs filling."

There was a faint smell of old leather, old wood – leather on padded seats that ran along two sides, polished wood panelling the walls (did you *call* them walls?) and in the great oak table fixed to the floor (did you call it the floor?) and in the small shutters for the brass-rimmed portholes. An oil lamp stood on the table, and lamps and storm lanterns hung from iron hooks in the blackened beams above.

"Oh *crikey!*" The whole thing was almost unbearable. He wished his friends could see him now – his mother, his football captain.

"There's berths forrard and aft," Mr Dallaker told him, "and galley and hold aft."

"If I could go to sea in this," said Ned with conviction, "just *once*, I should die happy. And talking of dying, Mr Dallaker, please could I see the log? The new one, I mean?"

He nodded, and opened one of the lockers beneath the padded seats. Ned could see several leather-covered volumes, big as dictionaries. Mr Dallaker looked back over his shoulder.

"Vol. One?" he asked. "Or Vol. Eight? First or last?"

"Oh first, please!"

"Sit here at the table, and I'll show you."

Fiony went round and sat on her father's other side.

"You don't see this often, do you, lass?" he said. "High days and holidays, that's all. Usually fetch it out Christmas." He raised his voice. "You coming, Nell?"

"You get on and show them," came her voice, "I'm coming!"

Mr Dallaker opened the book like a man who has never opened a book before.

"This," he said reverently, "is page one. First entry. Wrote by my grandfather and Fiony here's great-grandfather, one and the same. Captain Zed Dallaker."

"Z?" interrupted Ned. "What does Z stand for?"

"It don't stand," he replied, "for anything. Least, it did, but nobody remembers what. Some queer name picked from the Bible, we guess, which is full of queer names, with due respect. It's a good Dallaker name, Zed – bold-sounding."

"Oh it is," agreed Ned. "I just wondered, that's

all. Go on, Mr Dallaker. Did Captain Zed write all the entries?"

"From April 14th 1890 till 4th November 1932. When he died in Africa of the yellow fever. God rest his soul."

"God rest his soul," added Fiony.

"God rest his soul," said Ned, feeling it was expected of him. "Did he really? Die of yellow fever?"

"Was you wanting to look at this here log?" enquired Mr Dallaker.

"Oh, of course!" Ned cried. "Please go on. Can we read it? The writing's queer, isn't it? All slanted. And the ink's gone all brownish, or was that the colour ink they had in those days, to match the photographs? Can *you* read it, Mr Dallaker?"

"I was waiting," he said, "the opportunity. And the writing is copperplate. Best copperplate. Wrote the fanciest hand a Dallaker's ever had, Zed did – as far as known."

"Read it. Please."

"September 18th, 1897 0600 hours. Wind N.E. veering to east. Latitude 55.0°N., Longitude 2.50°E. Circled area in search of missing box."

"*The* box? The brass-bound box?"

"What had happened, see, was this. There was

this storm, off the Dogger, in a north-east gale, and Zed, thinking to save the ship's papers if the *Sea Queen* was to founder, fetches the box up, meaning to lash it to a spar."

"And he did, didn't he, Father," put in Fiony. "It says in the log, 'lashed the chest to a broad timber some eight feet long, that we might the more easily recover it when the seas abated'."

"Unless *they* went down, of course," said Ned.

"True sailors," said Mr Dallaker with dignity, "don't allow for going down. If the ship's to be lost, they take to the boats, and it was that very thing Zed was aiming to do when it happened."

"What happened?"

"When a wave," he replied, "according to Captain Zed who was an upright man, more than thirty feet in height, crashed on to the deck of the *Queen*. He himself was saved" – he tapped the yellowing pages of the log – "by virtue of hanging hard to the rigging. But when the wave had broke" – here he sighed deeply and shook his head – "the box was gone. Spar and all. Gone."

"Oh dammit!" cried Ned. "And if he'd left it down below it'd never've been lost at all!"

"And *then* the storm blows out! That's the real beauty of it – just like that!" He snapped his fingers. "Oh, that wave was a *villain*! I lie nights even now, brooding on that wave. Last of the storm and" – another snap – "gone! Hundreds of years of Dallaker history in the wink of an eye!"

"Was the Captain there?" asked Ned. "Does *he* remember?"

"A baby," replied Mr Dallaker. "Don't remember a thing."

He sounded faintly accusing, as if he thought mere infancy a poor excuse for such a lapse of memory. They sat silent, staring at the closely written page, picturing it all.

"Mr Dallaker," said Ned at last, "you keep mentioning treasure. D'ye mean *real* treasure – gold and silver, and such? Or do you just mean the logs? I mean, they are treasure in a way, aren't they?"

"Both," he replied. "Very hot on pirate ramming, some of the early Dallakers. 'Show a pirate a Dallaker, and he'll show you his tail' – that was how the saying went."

"Crikey," said Ned. "Gold moidores and doubloons. Pieces of eight."

"Oh, some of *them*," agreed Mr Dallaker.

"And necklaces and rings for Mother and me," cried Fiony. "Aren't there, Father?"

"Your mother and you," he said, "shall be queens. Though it seems queer to say it, and we've none of us hankered after the gold, not till now. There was a time when we'd have thrown the lot straight back to the fishes if we could only've had the logs."

"You could've gone to your rest, you mean," suggested Ned. "In a manner of speaking."

"But now – well, it's the treasure and all we're after. Gold, pearls, rubies, we'll need 'em all, or it's a life ashore for the *Queen* and the Dallakers. The end of the road. And that'd be the breaking of the old girl's heart."

There was silence. Ned tried to take in the enormity of what he had said.

"You mean never to go to sea again?" he cried. "*Never?* The *Sea Queen*?"

"Neither her," said Mr Dallaker, "nor us. There's work to be done on her – and costly work. She ain't seaworthy, not as she should be." He lowered his voice, Ned guessed as you might when talking about a loved relative who was sick unto death.

"But if we was to get that treasure – *and get it we will* – she shall have a refit worth a queen's ransom. And we'll take her round the Cape again, me boyos, and show her places she ain't seen for a hundred years, and she shall go to Fiony in her turn trimmed like a–"

"I'm last of the line, see!" cried Fiony.

"What? You? A *girl*? You'll be captain of the *Queen*?"

"Shan't, I, Father?" Fiony nodded.

"Well!" exclaimed Ned. "That beats all. Still," he shrugged, "I s'pose if you'd *like* that kind of a life . . ."

He wondered if it were possible to actually *die* of jealousy.

"So that's it," said Mr Dallaker heavily. He closed the book and absently stroked the cover with his thin, salt-bitten fingers. "No treasure – no sailing."

"But who else is after it?" cried Ned. The whole story had so many twists and turns that he could hardly keep up with it. "Who wrote those messages?"

"Ah. That would be You Know Who."

"But I don't!" cried Ned. "I don't!"

"Scavengers," said Mr Dallaker. "That's who."

Now Ned remembered.

"Inland beachcombers!"

"If you like. Though I don't. Scavengers. There's a name that fits 'em."

"Don't talk about them, Father!" said Fiony. "I

don't like to hear about them."

"Scared," thought Ned. "Fine captain she'll make!" The thought comforted him.

"What are you going to do?" he asked.

"Wait," replied Mr Dallaker. "Wait."

Again they sat silent in the darkening cabin. And staring at the scudding sky through a porthole Ned suddenly remembered where he was, and where he was supposed to be.

"I've got to go!" He started up just as Mrs Dallaker appeared with a plate in one hand and a jug in the other.

"I'm sorry, Mrs Dallaker. I've got to go. My friends will be expecting me."

"You take a bite to eat on the way, then," she said, proffering the plate.

"Oh *thanks.*" He took a wedge of jam sponge and made for the steps. He turned. The three of them were watching him, oddly identical with their thin faces and round eyes, and looking mildly surprised.

"Back tomorrow!" he said, and went.

The old Captain slept on the darkening beach. Ned crept softly past him, almost in awe of the green dreams that might be springing in his head at that very moment. At the top of the dunes he turned for a last glimpse of the *Sea Queen*, poised on land with seaward-pointing prow. Soon the portholes would beam with the light of lamps, then they would be shuttered and closed. And then, much later, there would be a night tide to comb.

Ned shivered, zipped up his anorak, and began to run towards supper and the Pickerings.

Chapter 7

A pendulum swung inside Ned's head. Dallaker Pickering Dallaker Pickering tick tock tick tock.

Down in their basement the Pickerings were waiting. Ned arranged his face in a way he hoped would suit them, half-rascally, half-sorry.

"I'm afraid I'm a bit late, Auntie," he said, managing the last word with hardly a tremor. After all, this was a place to stay. Without the Pickerings he would not have been here at all, in the middle of the kind of adventure he had never dared dream of.

"Got detained, did you, dear?" asked Mrs Pickering. "Met a friend, did you?"

"Oh, you know."

"I know," she almost crooned. "Auntie knows."

"Oh no, you don't," Ned thought. Aloud he said:

"Did you have a good day, Mr Pickering? Uncle?"

The newspaper seated in one of the lower, more comfortable chairs gave a brief shake of acknowledgement.

"In a minute, dear," said Mrs Pickering. "Your uncle's just running down the Deaths and Miscellaneous. Then he'll have his supper. We all will. You go along and tell Jack, will you?"

Ned went along the corridor and opened the door of "ours". In the near-darkness he could just make out Jack's form, prone on his bed. He switched on the light. Jack lay with his back turned and did not move.

"Feeling all right?" Ned enquired.

Grunt.

"Perhaps that's why they wanted company for him," Ned thought. "Lost his powers of speech. Doesn't he ever speak?"

"Supper's ready," he said.

"O.K. I'm *coming*."

He pulled himself up, white-faced and blinking, and swung his legs over the side of the bed, showering sand on to the lino.

"What a life!" he said, and went straight past Ned and back towards the living-room.

Mrs Pickering was dishing up in the scullery. Ned noticed that there were four motley places set out at the table and another on a brilliantly painted tin tray. Set out on the tray were a knife, fork and spoon – all matching – and a napkin in a wooden ring. Mrs Pickering caught his stare.

"For Mr Blagger, dear," she said. "Taking his meals in his room. Going to take it along for me, are you, when it's ready?"

"All right." Ned was glad that Mr Blagger *was* going to keep himself to himself. "He's welcome to himself," he thought.

"Ever so taken by you, he was," she went on, "for all he caught hardly a glimpse of you."

She was scooping overdone sausages out of the frying pan. These were followed by dollops of watery mashed potatoes that flattened as they hit the plates.

"Soaked peas, Jack," she remarked, almost gaily, and snatched up another pan. "And now, dear, if you'll just run along with this to Mr Blagger's room? You'll knock on the door, won't you?"

Ned picked up the tray.

"Second on the left?"

"That's right. Mind how you go."

On Mr Blagger's door, a note was pinned. Written in large black capitals were the words KNOCK AND WAIT. Ned transferred the tray to the crook of one elbow while he managed a quick knock. There was no answer. The lodger, perhaps, had fallen asleep. If so, Ned reflected, it would perhaps be all right if he used his foot next time. He had just swung back his right foot for the kick when the door was flung suddenly open.

"Oh!" Ned nearly overbalanced, tray and all. "I was just bringing you your supper."

Mr Blagger was looking at Ned a shade more searchingly than he was *used* to being looked at.

"You are a good boy," he said at length. "I daresay."

He made no attempt to take the tray, so Ned stretched his arms right out, offering it. Mr Blagger stepped aside.

"On the table, if you please."

Ned went past him into the room and had a swift impression of what was almost luxury in this particular basement. He noticed a dark-green velvety table-cover, easy chair, rugs, lamps with shades – a fire! All this he had taken in before finding himself back in the passage and the door firmly closed behind him.

"Phew!" He returned to the scullery to find that the Pickerings had started their meal without ceremony – indeed, had almost finished. They ate as they did everything else – in quick yet stealthy movements, as if they were creeping up on something, stalking.

Ned, despite the slab of cake, was hungry.

"That's right," said Mrs Pickering, her mouth full. "You get stuck in. Like sausages, do you?"

Ned gulped and nodded. He did, usually.

"Cooking suit you, does it?" she asked after refilling her mouth.

"Oh yes," Ned lied. "Very nice."

"That's right. Home cooking."

Her words reminded Ned.

"Did you remember to post the letter to my mother?" he asked.

She threw up her hands, knife and fork included.

"As if I wouldn't!" she cried.

"Oh thanks! Perhaps I'll get one from her tomorrow."

The thought was warming. Between the extraordinary worlds of the Dallakers and the Pickerings it was good to know that the ordinary life was still there, still existed, somewhere.

"Pass the bottle!"

Ned started. Bottle? For an instant he saw it in his mind's eye, was whipped straight out of that stark scullery and back on to the tide line.

"*Sauce* bottle!" It was Jack, looking almost alive, eyes fixed on Ned's face, thin arm outstretched.

"Please," said Mrs Pickering.

"Bottle, please."

Ned pushed over the sauce, which seemed to him to be perfectly within Jack's reach, anyway.

"And what you want with sauce when you've only half a sausage left I don't know," observed his mother. "Sauce on *bread*, you'd eat, if I didn't watch you. Put your plates in the sink, boys. We'll wash up later."

"Fetch the beer, Mother," said Mr Pickering, pushing his plate over to Jack. "Let's crack a bottle."

Again the dry sand, the green glass flower unfurling . . . GET OUT . . .

"You rascal," said Mrs Pickering half-heartedly, rummaging in a cupboard under the sink and snatching out first a large, dusty brown bottle, then two equally dusty glasses. She gave them a quick wipe on her pinafore and set them on the table.

"Mr Pickering's starting on Miscellaneous tomorrow," she confided in Ned. "Aren't you, Arthur? Just for the meantime."

Ned hoped that she was not going to suggest that he went Knocking. Ordinarily, he would have jumped at the chance, but he was finding it difficult to go through the motions of ordinary day-to-day living at all, away from the *Sea Queen* and the Dallakers.

"Jack'll give him a hand," she continued, "and then tomorrow night" – she raised her frothing glass – "there'll be sorting! I ain't sure I shan't miss all that, Arthur, when we've gone up in the world."

"We ain't gone up yet," observed Mr Pickering, wiping his mouth with the back of his hand.

"Ah, but we shall! We all shall – and Ned shall, too, shan't you?"

"Er – yes, Mrs – er, Auntie," he said.

"I was telling Mr Pickering how you said you'd help us, and he was not one scrap surprised – said he could tell straight off that you were the kind of boy'd want to help, didn't you, Arthur? And have you made any friends yet on the beach, did you say?"

"Oh, you know. I spoke to one or two people."

"Ah, you would – nice friendly boy like you. And when you was talking to these people, did you happen to have mentioned who you was staying with?"

"No." Ned was surprised. "Nobody asked."

It seemed to him that Mr and Mrs Pickering exchanged swift glances over their glasses.

"Ah – nobody asked. They wouldn't, would they? No reason why they should ask."

"No – no reason at all."

"So if anybody *was* to ask you," pursued Mrs Pickering, *worrying* the subject, "it'd be because they *had* a reason? Wouldn't it?" She sounded triumphant.

"Well – yes, I suppose it would."

"And so it'd be better" – she was almost purring now – "if you wasn't to tell them."

"Or better still," put in Mr Pickering, "made up a tale. Eh, Jack?"

Jack did not answer. He was regarding Ned with his usual malevolent stare. He seemed to be in a perpetual state of *grudgingness.*

"All right," said Ned, eager to bring the conversation to an end. "I will, then. Make up a tale."

"That's right!" cried Mrs Pickering. "We knew you was a rascal at heart! Everyone is!"

With two words she peopled the whole world with Pickerings.

"Now, dear, you just run along and see if there's anything else Mr Blagger wants. Mind you knock."

Reluctantly Ned went back along the passage, and this time when he knocked he heard Mr Blagger's voice almost immediately. "Come in!"

He was sitting at the table with his back to the door and did not turn his head or speak.

"Mrs Pickering wondered if there was anything else you wanted?"

Mr Blagger was deliberately turning over playing cards on the fringed velvet cloth. He seemed to be playing patience.

"There's no end to the things I want," he said slowly. The remark was so unexpected that it took Ned several seconds to realise that this was the answer to his question.

"No end," he repeated, and began to sweep the cards together and stack them. He shuffled and then began to deal again with his thick white fingers. It seemed to Ned that if Mr Blagger *really* wanted no end of things, playing patience was an odd way to set about getting them.

"Shall I take your tray, then?"

The white fingers moved over the green cloth. The head nodded. Ned picked up the tray and made for the door.

"Wait!"

Ned turned back. Still Mr Blagger did not turn his head.

"Have you been given instructions?"

"Instructions? No! At least – well, they did say something about not telling people where I was staying."

The head nodded and still the hands moved.

"Do as they say."

"Oh, I will."

"Wait for further instructions."

Ned, startled, nodded, realised that Mr Blagger could not see him, blurted out the two words "All right" and next minute, without quite knowing how, was outside the door. He stood staring at the printed notice. The black letters seemed to jump out from the card, KNOCK AND WAIT. His heart began to jerk unevenly. GO AWAY . . . GET OUT . . . Those black irregular capitals . . .

He turned away and went into his own room. It was lit dimly by a sodium street lamp slanting from above. He placed the tray quietly on the floor before flinging himself on his bed, shivering with cold and terror.

He was among Scavengers.

Chapter 8

Ned took the letter into his room to read. He had the house to himself. Mr Pickering and Jack had already gone off on their rounds. Mrs Pickering had gone out shopping and Mr Blagger had not appeared at all that morning.

"Mr B don't want disturbing, dear," Mrs Pickering had told him. "Nor he don't want any breakfast, either."

Ned had tiptoed past the closed door. Now he sat on the edge of the bed and tore open the envelope.

"Dear Ned, Thank you for your letter (so she *had* posted it – after reading it first?). I'm glad that you seem to be settling down well and have already made a friend. I expect it's nice, too, to have a boy of your own age to do things with, and great fun to share a room with him. (Ned grimaced.) I've often worried about your not having enough companionship and perhaps when you are both a bit older and it won't matter so much about my being out at work all day, Jack will be able to come and stay with *us*. I miss seeing you when I get back in, and so does Duke – he keeps going and lying on your bed in the mornings just as if you were still there. Well, dear, I'd love to write more, but I've promised to go and baby-sit for Mr and Mrs Phillips tonight, so I'll have to stop. Have a lovely holiday and enjoy yourself. All my love, Mother. P.S. I should keep woollies on while you're on the beach – I know how cold it can be."

Ned stared at the letter. He had been almost able to hear his mother's voice as he read it, but oddly, instead of being a comfort, it seemed to make things worse. Its brightness, its sheer ordinariness, cut the ground from under his feet. For a brief, panic-stricken time last night he had been tempted to run out of the house to find a 'phone kiosk and ring the neighbour's number she had given him in case of emergency, and tell her everything.

Now, sitting on the edge of the bunk, he saw clearly the sheer impossibility of communicating to her (especially over the telephone) the strange plight he was in. What did *she* know of the kind of worlds inhabited by the Dallakers and the Pickerings? What had *he* known of them until now?

"I can't tell her," he decided, and folded up the letter. "I can't tell anyone."

He dared not even tell the Dallakers. He himself felt as if he had known them all his life, but it was a mere two days since he had first met them. And they were a people apart, dwellers of the sea and shore, and he was chained to the land and houses. They had their own mysterious paths and he knew already that he could never hope to follow them. The most he could hope for was a brief glimpse of their strange world, a brief friendship with them, and – at best, at breathtaking best – a brief part to play in making their dearest dreams come true.

But if they should discover that he was in the midst of their enemies, living among Scavengers – what then?

"And what can the Pickerings do, in any case," he thought. "After all, they're only land

Scavengers. What do they know about the sea? The old Captain – he knows *everything*, he said so himself. Moons, tides – *and* dreams, whatever that means. The Beachcombers catch the tide morning and night and they're always there, down on the shore. But the Pickerings spend all day grubbing round on shore for their Miscellaneous or Chairs or whatever it is, and they're snoring here while Mr Dallaker's combing the night tide."

Ned sat and he thought, and he thought not only of the Pickerings but of Mr Blagger, dealing cards by the hour in his small back room. And the longer he thought, the less he understood. And the less he understood, the less he liked it. In the end, he did the only thing possible. He put on his beach shoes, tucked the football under his arm, and went out – banging the door to lock it as Mrs Pickering had instructed him.

With the very first deep breath of fresh air he felt courage returning. He even took a backward glance at Number Eleven, and it looked so smugly red-brick and net-curtained and so exactly the twin of its neighbours that he almost laughed out loud with relief.

All the way down to the sea he kept sniffing the cold, mackerel-smelling air, and then the sun came out. Women were scrubbing steps and carpets were being beaten. Easter was only a week away and suddenly everything must be made clean.

"They've just timed it right for their Miscellaneous," Ned thought. "Perhaps they'll make their fortune at *that*, and never mind the treasure."

In any case, once down the hard, wet pullover and on to the great, sunlit beach with its giant shadows and sea more blue than grey, the Pickerings faded and shrank till it seemed ridiculous that he should ever have been afraid of them. He walked the tide line, beachcomber-wise, though he knew full well that the Dallakers would have been there before him and the pickings small. The line was higher than it had been the day before, and he remembered what Mr Dallaker had said about the "spring tides rising".

Far away at the sea's edge he could see one or two groups of children kicking balls, their long shadows raking about them. Most of the local children seemed hardly to bother with the beach at all.

"They would," he thought, "if they knew about the treasure."

The mile to the bank of dunes seemed short today. As he began to climb, he felt the familiar thud of his heart in his throat. He could never quite believe that the *Sea Queen* was really there, that she was not some kind of private mirage, a trick of the light. Though he had trodden her decks and visited her deep, wood-smelling depths, he knew that if, today, he were to find her gone, within a few weeks he would not be able to believe that she had existed at all.

She was there, wreathed in smoke and gulls, pointed shadows sharp-edged on the sands anchoring her, *making* her real.

"Ahoy!" he shouted and heard an answering call. Fiony appeared round the stern and ran to meet him, barefoot and kicking up the sand.

"Come on, quick! We've been talking about you!"

"Me? Why?" He tried to hide his pleasure that the Dallakers should think of him in his absence just as he thought of them.

"You'll see. Father'll tell you. Come on."

The rest of the Dallakers were sitting round on deck, all busy with ropes or nets.

"Here he is, Father!"

"That I see," he replied. And they all said "Good morning", then, so formally that Ned guessed it was out of respect to the Captain rather than himself.

"Nothing on the night tide, I suppose?" he asked. "Silly question – can't have been, or you wouldn't all be sitting here."

"Right we shouldn't" agreed Mr Dallaker. "Out there's where we'd be–" he pointed to the horizon – "clear and away."

It was true, Ned thought. They would not even have waited to say goodbye.

"We've been talking about you this morning, young Ned," went on Mr Dallaker.

"Fiony said. What about me?"

"We was wondering, just *wondering*, how much you was a friend?"

"Oh *very* much! Very much indeed! I'd do anything to help you – anything!"

"Ah. I was coming round to that. Helping. It ain't easy for us, see, asking help. We've never been used much to land-dwellers – could take 'em or leave 'em, so to speak. And mostly leave 'em," he added.

"And what *can* I do to help?"

"I don't really know that we ought to ask him." Mrs Dallaker's face was puckered. "We don't know for sure what it might lead him into."

"Oh go on!" Ned cried. "Do!"

"I'll ask," announced Mr Dallaker, with the air of a man who has finally made up his mind. "What we wondered, was this. You living on land, see, could be a rare help to us, on account of a certain fact. And that fact is" – he paused – "the fact of *certain other parties* being land-dwellers."

Ned was silent.

"If you take my point."

"The Scavengers." With an effort Ned met the other's eye.

"In one," agreed Mr Dallaker. "Got it in one. The nub of the problem, as I've said before, being that the Scavengers see us, but we don't see *them*."

"Don't even know for sure that they're about," his wife reminded him.

"Oh yes. We know that, Nell, though we don't *like* to know it. And after last night, we know for downright certain."

"Last night?" Ned's voice was almost a squeak. "What happened last night?"

"There might be nothing in it, at all," said Mrs Dallaker. "Don't you go frightening the boy. It's none of it to do with him at all, if it comes to that."

"But it is! I want to know! Please!"

"Well, then," said Mr Dallaker, "what happened last night is that footmarks was seen."

"Which might have nothing at all to do with it," interrupted Mrs Dallaker again, determined it seemed to put the damper on anything that might suggest excitement or adventure. Ned noticed that her own thin neck and cheeks were red. *She* was excited. "Those footprints, Matthew, are altogether too big for Scavengers – least, for the Scavengers *we're* thinking of. There's no Pickering got feet *that* big."

Pickering. Now the name had been spoken. It was true – even here on the bright, windy beach, it was all true. He had thought he had buried the Pickerings back at Number Eleven Bakers Road, pushed them away into a separate compartment of his mind and forgotten them, as you did with a nightmare.

"Feet," Mr Dallaker was saying, "feet, Nell, can be fitted into boots twice too big for them if needs be, to deceive. And if there's one thing a Scavenger's better fit to do than a Beachcomber, it's deceive."

Ned, picturing Mr Pickering clumping over the darkened sands at dead of night in boots several sizes too big, let out a high, nervous laugh that was more than half a shriek. The others looked at him, surprised.

The Captain spoke for the first time.

"Before any more's said, hear what the boy says."

They continued to look at him, alive as wires now and sharp-eyed, and Ned knew that the moment of truth had come. He did not make a decision at all – there was no time. He forgot, too, the decision he had already made earlier that morning. That was then, and this was *now*, and things clearer here than they had seemed there, alone in the dim, silent basement.

"I'll help," he said, watching their taut, salt-bitten faces. "But there's something I've got to tell you."

They waited.

"I know the Pickerings."

No one spoke.

"I'm living with them."

Now it had been said, and even seeing their faces, aghast and unbelieving, he was glad, because everything that was said from now onward could at least be the truth.

"The bottle," said Mr Dallaker heavily at last. "That bottle. And the message in the sand."

"*No!*" Ned, in turn, was aghast. "No! It wasn't me! I didn't know anything about it. I didn't even realise that the Pickerings *were* Scavengers, not till last night. Please, Mr Dallaker, you must believe me. I didn't know!"

"He's telling the truth," the Captain said.

"I am – oh, I am! And I *hate* the Pickerings, all of them, and Mr Blagger, too, and–"

He told them everything. It was marvellous to confess in that rinsed and empty air, to bring the Pickerings out of their dark world and into that bright sea wind. As he talked he saw them bleach and fade, like photographs over-exposed. He talked about the advertisement, about the basement full of broken chairs, the mysterious references to "going up in the world", and hints that Ned himself was to help them. And as he talked pictures floated before him and fell into place – the sand spilling from Jack's shoes the night before, the talk of "bottles" at supper, the warning that Ned should "invent a tale" if asked where he was staying.

"And it was *Jack* put that bottle there," he finished, suddenly certain of it. "He was supposed to've been out on the van, but he'd got sand in his shoes. And it was him that wrote in the sand – the writing was the same as on Mr Blagger's door, and – who *is* Mr Blagger?"

"Mr Blagger, I should guess," replied Mr

Dallaker, "is Mr Smith. Or Mr Brown. Or Mr Jones."

"What do you *mean*?" Ned was beside himself now, irretrievably committed, and glancing all the time at the dunes behind, dreading a glimpse of a face or movement of the grass that would betray the presence of an enemy, a watcher.

"I mean that he ain't Mr Blagger, nor Mr Anyone Else. Playing the cards, you say, and lying low?"

"He hasn't even been out of his room this morning!"

"He ain't been out this morning," said Mr Dallaker, "because he's been treading the beach all night. Chief Scavenger, that's who. And cleverer than the whole pack of Pickerings put together."

"Chief Scavenger? How many *are* there, then?"

"How many crabs on this beach?" countered Mr Dallaker. "How many shells or jellies or stones? The world's full of failed Beachcombers."

"Then how did you know it was the Pickerings in particular?" Ned was almost as confused as ever.

"Because the Pickerings, I regret to say," replied Mr Dallaker, "are related."

"Distantly," put in the Captain. He removed

his pipe from his mouth purposely to say the word, evidently thinking the effort well worth while.

"Related? The Pickerings? But they're nothing *like* you!"

"That," said Mr Dallaker, "I am fully glad to hear you say."

The Captain removed his pipe again.

"In the Dallaker family," he observed, "water is thicker than blood, as you might say."

"Nicely put," said Mr Dallaker. "Sea water, as you say, thicker than blood. And friendship" – he looked directly at Ned now – "friendship thicker than either?"

"Yes! Yes! You just tell me what you want me to do, and I'll do it. Anything!"

"It ain't so much a question of doing," he said, "as of watching. Watching and listening."

"A sort of spy in the camp?"

He nodded.

"Evens things out a bit, see. Makes things fair. They see us, we don't see them. But *you* see them – and we're all square."

"The only thing is," Ned said, "that I've got a feeling they're going to get me to spy on you. They keep going on about me helping them. But that'd make it even better, wouldn't it? I could pretend to be spying on you, and then tell them all the wrong things. I'd be a kind of counter-spy."

"What's that?" asked Fiony.

Ned stared.

"Don't you ever watch television?"

"No," she said, and in the same instant Ned had a picture of the *Sea Queen* with an aerial fixed to her mast, and grinned at Fiony.

"Silly question," he admitted.

"You're a brave boy," said Mrs Dallaker, and a smile lit her thin, dark face. "We shouldn't be asking you."

"My mother would certainly have a fit," agreed Ned, and really did feel a hero, sitting there among the Dallakers on their marvellous, sea-battered boat, plotting, planning the rout of the Scavengers. The very salt smell of the air made the possibility of treasure and triumph seem only a step – a wave – away. He looked round at them and saw that they were all looking at him and that he was unmistakably there right at the centre of it all.

"Oh crikey," he said. "*Crikey.*"

Chapter 9

Back at Number Eleven Bakers Road the pendulum swung again. Dallaker Pickering Dallaker Pickering tick tock tick tock. And now and then a new note sounding – Blagger.

But it was broad daylight even in the basement and lucky for Ned that the Pickerings chose now as the time to come out into the open. Night would have cornered him.

The minute he entered the living-room he could see at a glance that Mr Pickering and Jack were back from their Knocking. The broken chairs were all stacked in the far corner, and next to them was a pile of what Ned supposed was the morning's haul of Miscellaneous. At first sight it looked interesting – as other people's rubbish always does. Books, clothes, jugs, tables, cricket bat, roller skates . . . He had just started to take in the details – the crack straight down the centre of the bat, the wheels missing from the skates – when Mrs Pickering emerged from the scullery.

"See it!" She waved towards the heap of rubbish. "Three hours Knocking, and look at it all!"

"To her," Ned thought, amazed by the revelation, "*that's* treasure!"

For a moment she was even likeable, brimming happiness. The Dallakers themselves, discovering at last a brass-bound box on the tide line, could not have been happier.

"And they're going out again!" she cried. "Think of it! Oh, there'll be sorting tonight, dear! See this!"

She darted foward and snatched up a green crocheted jumper, holding it up against her grubby overall.

"*Beautiful!* And this – do for you, dear – play on the beach with Jack!" She prodded the split bat with her foot.

"That'll be the day," he thought. But he knew that she really believed in it – that she saw the

Pickerings' whole life being somehow magically changed by that little heap of junk. She really could, at that moment, see Jack and himself running and shouting together on the beach, boon companions, while she herself perhaps sat nearby, wearing the green crocheted jumper, smiling and ladylike.

"You can live like a lord off the things other people throw out." It was as if she had read his thought. "But mustn't look now, must we? Spoil the fun for tonight. Sorting . . ."

He followed her into the scullery where Jack and his father were sitting with empty plates before them.

"Didn't mind us starting?" Mr Pickering seemed cheerful, as if his spirits, at any rate, had not been "lowered" by a morning's Knocking. "Get the lad his dinner, Mother. Jack 'nd me'll have to be off."

Ned, as he seated himself opposite Jack, saw a quick nod and frown pass from father to son. He looked up and found Jack's pale eyes on him.

"Saw you with that girl again today," he said, so unexpectedly that Ned actually felt himself start.

"Oh! You mean Fiony."

"With the whole gang, wasn't you?" Jack went on. "That Dallaker gang."

"Dunno about a gang," said Ned. "More a family, I thought."

He was conscious all the time of hints and glances flying like forked lightnings about him, of Mrs Pickering hovering, of a sense, yet again, that he had been cast in the lead part of a very bad and confusing play.

"Now you didn't mean that, did you, Jack?" Mrs Pickering was unable to contain herself any longer in mere hovering.

"He don't put things too well, dear." This to Ned. "Nerves, see. It's just that he says 'gang' with them being on opposite sides from us, see?"

"Opposite sides?" echoed Ned blankly. When he was playing a part he understood, he did it quite well.

"Them's Beachcombers. We're Scavengers." It was Jack again, "Lot of thieving sea gypsies!"

"You hush!" Mrs Pickering dealt Jack a smart blow on the side of his head, at the same time giving Ned her particular smile, which was a kind of swift stretching of the lips that had nothing to do with the rest of her face at all. (Or her hands either, evidently.)

"Just ain't too fond of Beachcombers," she

said. "We none of us is. Though I daresay they seemed human enough to you?"

"Seem all right," Ned mumbled.

"P'raps they are," put in Mr Pickering, "to an *outsider.* But to us, see, they're the *enemy.*"

"Meaning us harm," added Mrs Pickering. "Trying to stop us going up in the world, eh, Arthur?"

Ned, in his role of double spy, was so confused that he almost himself for a moment saw the Dallakers as The Enemy, because he could see so clearly that, from the Pickerings' point of view, that was exactly what they were.

"Never been any good in water gypsies," she went on. "Sailing about from pillar to post, never knowing where the next meal's coming from. Best thing Arthur's side of the family ever did, getting out of it. Getting ashore and a roof over their heads, and safe pickings. Related, you see, dear, though I hardly like to say so."

"I know," Ned *almost* found himself saying, but instead came out with:

"Related? I'd never have guessed it!" which was at least true, and which was exactly what he had been saying to the Dallakers only an hour or two ago.

"I hope I'm going to be able to keep this up,"

he thought. He *knew* whose side he was on, and yet to be in the very camp of the enemy, and hear their point of view, oddly blurred the issue, made things much less straightforward than they seemed.

"Guessed it?" Mrs Pickering half-shrieked. "I should hope not indeed! Thieving water gypsies!"

"You just hit me, ma, for saying that."

She did not even hear him.

"Mind you," she was saying, "only *distant*, aren't we, Arthur?"

The Pickerings were no more eager to claim relationship with the Dallakers than vice versa. The Pickerings, it became clearer and clearer, did not see themselves as villains at all.

"Perhaps villains never do," Ned thought, surprised by the thought and yet at the same time seeing how easily it could be true.

"We still ain't told him yet what we're after," pointed out Mr Pickering, laying his hands palm downward on the table as if electing himself chairman.

"Put him in the picture, Arthur, that's first thing!" she snapped back. "Got to put it to him *right*, remember?"

She had forgotten for the moment that Ned was there.

"Because if we get it *wrong*," she continued, "*he'll* want to know why!" A jerk of the head that was nowhere near in the direction of Mr Blagger and yet unmistakably *meant* Mr Blagger.

"Now, dear," back to Ned again, wheedling, "you remember, don't you, how you said you'd help?"

"Yes. Of course."

"And how we'd all go up in the world together – us, you and your dear mother?"

"I remember, Mrs – Auntie."

"There's a good boy!" she cried. Then, "And a rascal too!" hastily, as if rascaliness was going to be as necessary to their plans as goodness.

"*I'll* tell him," she said to Jack. "You sit quiet. Spoil everything, you would."

Jack raised his eyebrows and turned down his mouth in the same movement, and Ned felt sorry for him.

"Them Dallakers, see," she began, "is out to spike us. Is out to do us out of our lawful rights, see?"

"Not really," said Ned.

"There ain't altogether any need for all the

details," she went on. "It's a family matter, eh, Arthur?"

Mr Pickering nodded.

"What you might happen to hear them Dallakers mentioning," she said, "is the word 'treasure'. *Not"* – she put up a paw – hand – "not that there's any call for you to go getting excited about that, dear, as there ain't altogether all that *much* of it, and the share we shall be able to spare to you and your dear mother won't be under the heading of treasure. Just a neat little sum, dear, so when you hear the word 'treasure' spoke, just throw it a pinch of salt, will you?"

It seemed to Ned that if the treasure were quite as small as Mrs Pickering was making out, they were going to very great lengths to lay their hands on it. However, he could see that he was *meant* to believe that there was nothing very much to be excited about, so he looked as unexcited as he could and said "Just a little family nest-egg, I suppose," and was proud of the remark. It met with immediate approval from the Pickerings.

"*That's* it!" cried Mrs Pickering. "That's it exactly. And this little nest-egg, dear, is, as far as is known at present, afloat in the North Sea in a brass-bound box!"

This statement obviously called for some excitement, so Ned raised his eyebrows high and cried: "Whatever's it doing there?"

"Oh, *much* too much to go into, dear," she told him. "But I shall tell you whose fault it is, and no mistake at all need be made about that!"

"The Dallakers?"

"Oh, Arthur," she shook her head. "*What* a needle! What a sharp boy we've got here. What did I tell you?"

And she shook her head at her own son, as if to bid him mark how bright a boy *could* be, if he tried. This, oddly, made Ned feel less proud of himself.

"Now, all we want you to do, dear," she went on, "is to give us word what you see and hear on the beach. To tell us whatever is spoke on the matters of treasure and brass-bound boxes, and above all things" – she wagged a finger – "above all, not a whisper of a word to 'em of who you're stopping with!"

Ned, in his turn, nodded. In many ways, nods were safer than words. She let out a long, satisfied breath.

"There we are, then, Arthur, Jack! All done. All in the treasure hunt together now – not *real* treasure, of course!"

"Good! Good!" Mr Pickering rose briskly. "Off we go, Jack. Knock, knock! 'Good afternoon, Madam, I wonder if we can be of any service to you in your Spring Cleaning? Take off any old clutter out of your way, perhaps, or– Come *on*, Jack!"

"You have a word with Mr Blagger on your way out!" she called after them. "Remember? And knock, mind!"

"Knock!" Ned heard Mr Pickering's disgusted voice. "Knock!"

"And you'll be getting off to the beach, won't you, dear?" she said to Ned, in a way that somehow made it clear that he had better.

As it happened, he could hardly wait.

Chapter 10

Ned raced towards the *Sea Queen's* bay, propelled by triumph and excitement. It seemed to him that the game was now as good as won – he had hoodwinked the Pickerings.

The Dallakers themselves were delighted by the news. But their delight was guarded, and with Mr Dallaker's very first words Ned felt his own jubilation beginning to ebb.

"That's put *them* off course, then," he said. "For the time being."

"But they'll never find out! Why should they? They know I'm coming down here every day, but they *want* me to! And how could they possibly know what we're saying?"

Ned glanced as he spoke towards the dunes beyond, and was reassured that his words were out of carrying distance.

"You don't shake off Scavengers so easy," said the Captain. "Mind your step."

"Oh, I will," Ned said, and remembered reluctantly how near he had come already to giving himself away to the Pickerings – more than once.

"Might not be for long, anyway – might it, Grandad?" said Fiony.

"How long?" Ned asked.

There was a long pause before the Captain replied, so long that Ned began to think that there was to be no answer, that he had asked the wrong question again.

"Don't believe overly in pinning things down exact," he said at last. "And as for the sea – she *can't* be pinned down. I ain't speaking by the almanack."

"Could be tonight, couldn't it?" wondered Fiony softly. She had thrown herself back and lay there loosely combing the sand with her fingers. "I think it'll be on the night tide, when it comes."

"If it comes," said her mother.

"No, Nell," said Mr Dallaker. "We don't say

'if', not any more. We say 'when'. It's certain."

She wrinkled her face at him but Ned, catching the look, saw that she too was certain, despite what she said. He threw himself down at Fiony's side and in doing so his hand brushed against her soft arm and he shivered suddenly and thought:

"She's real. They all are."

"Your hand felt cold," she said idly.

He lay silent at her side, listening not to the murmuring voices of the other Dallakers, but to the gulls and the distant roar of the sea. The cold sand thundered by his ear. He opened his eyes and saw the *Sea Queen*'s masts pointed into the depthless white light of the sky.

"If time could stand still," he thought, "this would be the time when I wanted it to . . ."

Almost, it did. He certainly could not have told how long he lay there, pounded by light and the sea's roar, and when Fiony touched his arm and he sat up, suddenly, he was dizzy and blurred as if he had woken from deep sleep.

"Crikey, Fiony," he heard his own voice say, though he had no intention of speaking, "I tell you, I'd give anything if I could go voyaging on the *Sea Queen*. Anything."

She shrugged.

"P'raps you will. Anyway, you can get a boat of your own, when you're grown up."

Ned was silent.

"Will you, d'ye think?"

"I might." Though he did not see how. Most grown-ups he knew didn't go sailing off on voyages, beachcombing. They went and worked in offices or shops, and lived in neat houses, all in rows.

"Or you could marry *me*." She was mischievous now, standing over him, the wind catching her hair and skirts. "I'm next Captain of the *Sea Queen*."

He did not answer.

"Well, don't you think I'm pretty?"

He looked away and felt his face redden.

"Of course."

"All right, then. I will."

"Will what?"

"Marry you."

He sprang up now, aghast.

"But I didn't *ask* you!"

"Oh, *Ned*! Can't you play games? Come on, catch me!"

She started off up the beach towards the dunes, and he went after her, still dizzy and feeling the sand pull oddly at his feet as if they had been made weightless.

"Race you!"

Just as he was about to put a hand to her shoulder she collapsed at his feet, breathless and laughing.

"I didn't know it *was* a race," he said.

"Oh you *did*! I said it. Race you!"

"You didn't say where to. I was giving you a start. With being a girl," he added.

"With being a girl!" She was mocking him now. "Who's going to be Captain?"

Ned could see the *Sea Queen* over her shoulder, beautifully curved yet solid, and pictured her launched, sails wet and filled with wind, spray whitening her bows. He almost groaned aloud.

"When you go" – again he found himself saying something without even meaning to – "don't go without me knowing. Please."

She stared at him.

"What? Even at night? It's clammy and dark down here nights, you know."

"I must see her. Actually afloat. Sailing."

"We shall go out on the same tide as the treasure comes in. And it'll be night. I know it." She too was staring at the *Queen* now, lips slightly parted, eyes enormous, and he almost suffocated with jealousy.

"Oh *dammit*!" he cried, and flung away from her, up the dunes, pulling savagely at the grasses to haul himself up, feeling his hands smart.

"Listen, Ned! Wait!" She was coming after him, fast and nimble. "If you really want to see her sail, you can!"

He stopped and faced her.

"What do you mean?"

"You *will*," she insisted. "Because you'll *know* she's sailing. Something'll tell you. Even in your sleep."

"Oh *that*!"

He started off again, but she caught him by the arm.

"Really! It works. Grandad'll tell you. How do you think *he* knows the treasure's coming?"

He was silent, and filled with a sudden hope, despite himself. After all, why should it not be true? Everything else to do with the Dallakers was equally impossible, yet that was true.

"You'll see," she said. "You'll be there – if you want it bad enough."

"Come on," he said. "What's on the other side of here?"

He started again into the dunes that ringed

the inland edge of the bay, and had hardly begun the climb when a figure rose suddenly from behind a mound about twenty yards to the right. A white face turned to look backward. Jack Pickering.

"Hey!" Ned shouted. How long had he been there? How close had he been? Had he heard?

Jack turned and faced him, still at a distance.

"Hello!" Ned called, forcing friendliness. "Didn't know you were there."

"Don't you dare say my name!" Jack shouted back. "Don't you dare! You remember what ma said!"

"Who's that?" asked Fiony.

"Just someone I know."

To his surprise, Jack, instead of heading back towards the town, began to advance towards them.

"I know who *she* is," he leered. "Finny, that's who!"

"Fiony." Ned and Fiony spoke together.

"Finny. Finny Haddock. What's that old heap down there?"

He jerked a thumb towards the *Sea Queen*.

"What's that, Finny? A wreck?"

"You stop it!" she cried furiously, stamping a foot in the sand. "You get away! *You* tell him," this to Ned, "he's your friend. Tell him to get away."

"He's not my friend," said Ned. "I told you, I hardly know him. Come on, *we'll* go."

He turned, but Fiony stood her ground, captainwise.

"Not while he's there. Let *him* go."

"Hark at Finny! What are you – a gypsy?"

Ned began to move towards him.

"Listen, you leave her alone. *You* remember."

"You shut up!" Jack's face was whiter than ever now, and distorted. "Rotten little goody goody. You can *keep* your dirty little gypsy, and–"

He did not finish the sentence. Ned, in a few bounds, was at him, fists up, and Jack, caught off guard, stumbled sideways. Next minute he was up. He took a swinging blow at Ned's head, missed, and himself received the full force of Ned's fist, right in the eye. He let out a yell of rage and pain and threw himself back at Ned, pushing him violently in the chest. Ned, poised on the slope, lost his balance and fell, as if in slow motion. He heard Fiony scream. Then Jack was on him, they were locked and wrestling in deadly earnest.

"Stop it! Stop it!" He could hear Fiony screaming and felt a hard fist glance past his ear.

He saw her wild face above Jack's head and then her fists came down again, raining blows on his opponent's head and shoulders.

"Leave – him!" he gasped. With a tremendous effort he heaved Jack's weight sideways and then they were both rolling down the slope together, still locked, and when they reached the bottom, this time Ned was on top. He drew up his legs and straddled Jack's chest, pinning down his arms.

"Traitor!" Jack's face, flushed for the first time since Ned had known him, was only a foot away from his own.

"You started it. If I let you go, are you going?"

"I'm *going*," said Jack between his teeth. "I'm going. Straight home. And you wait. Just you wait!"

With a sudden movement Ned released Jack's arm and leapt backwards.

"Go on, then, go! And you remember who started it!"

Jack scrambled to his feet and went past Ned without a word. They watched him go. The back of his hair and jacket were furred with sand.

"Who was it?" asked Fiony again. "It wasn't a–"

"Yes. Pickering. Scavenger. Jack Pickering."

"Are you hurt?" she edged round him, staring. "I thought he'd *kill* you."

"I'm all right." He still stared after Jack's retreating figure. "The thing is, did he *hear*?"

"A relation!" She too was staring now. "*Him!* Ugh!"

"I've got to go back there," Ned said.

"He started it."

"They can't do anything," Ned told himself. Even if Jack had heard, and told them, there was nothing they could do. "I'll just pack and go. They can't stop me."

"I'm glad you hit him. You hit him really hard, right in the eye."

Jack was out of sight now, on his way back to Bakers Road to report. Because the Pickerings had sent him there to spy, that was certain. All along he had been spying, all the time he was supposed to be out with his father on his rounds.

"They never really trusted me," Ned thought. "And now they probably know for certain."

He was conscious that his knuckles hurt, and there was a pain in his left shoulder.

"I thought you were marvellous," said Fiony. "Let's go and tell Father."

They faced back towards the sea, gone grey again with the weather.

"Funny," said Ned, "how the wind round here always smells of fish. Mackerel."

"Sea wind. This is nothing. Grandpa says in his day there was a smell of fish in St. Ives used to stop the church clock!"

"Oh come off it!" He laughed despite himself. "What did it stop at? Hake o'clock?"

"Race you!" She set off again, her voice floating back over her shoulder. "And this time don't say I didn't tell you! Race you!"

Chapter 11

Ned slackened his pace once he was over the pullover, and walked slowly through the town, really looking at it for the first time. It did not seem like a real seaside place at all – not like the ones where he had spent other holidays. It was as red brick and dull, once you left the beach behind, as any small inland town – duller, in fact, because there seemed to be so little life and movement. The whole place seemed to be so quiet, it seemed to be holding its breath. Perhaps it was – waiting for Easter and the summer season, for life to flow into it from the outside.

He had a sudden wild impulse to cup his hands to his mouth and bawl at the top of his voice

"Treasure! Treasure!"

Would the net curtains twitch, doors fly open, the streets be all at once alive with the hidden people? Would they lock up their shops and houses and go stampeding down to the sea's edge for a sight of the impossible, or would they merely look up for a moment, shrug, and go on with business as usual?

Two worlds, Ned thought. Here the certain, workaday town filled with ticking clocks and people talking about the weather that scarcely touched them under their safe red tiles. And there, beyond the moaning, wind-flattened grasses, the sea, harnessed not to clocks but to the moon and winds, making its own rhythm, carrying the weather on its back.

Two worlds, and he between them. Pickering Dallaker Pickering Dallaker tick tock tick tock. Blagger.

"And I choose the Dallakers," he told himself. "Whatever happens. The Dallakers and the *Sea Queen.*"

Mr Pickering's van was standing outside the house. They would all be there, waiting for him.

The living-room was empty, but he could hear pots rattling in the scullery. The pile of Miscellaneous had doubled in size and he hoped that this, at least, would have made Mrs Pickering mellow. He took a deep breath and went into the scullery. She was there alone, and there was no sign of a recent meal or of one in preparation. She whipped round from the sink.

"Oh. You're back, then."

"Yes."

She took a hard look at him.

"*You* ain't got no black eye, then."

"No." He felt apologetic, almost wishing that he *had*, feeling himself cast immediately as the villain of the piece, without so much as a scratch to show.

"I hope Jack's not too bad. I didn't mean to get him in his eye."

"For a black eye that wasn't *meant*," she observed sourly, "it's the best *I've* ever seen."

"Oh dear. Is it really? I'm very sorry, Mrs Pickering, I honestly didn't mean it."

"Black eye here and there won't do Jack any harm," she returned. "There's other things we've to worry about besides black eyes."

Again she took a hard look at him. Something in her manner had changed, of that he felt certain. He could not exactly put his finger on it. It was as if before she had been pretending to like him, and now she was pretending to pretend to like him. He himself was playing a double bluff, and some instinct now seemed to tell him that she was doing the same.

At any rate so far, it seemed, so good. She was evidently not going to fly at him or turn him out of the house or even – and this was one possibility that had occurred to him earlier – lock him up, keep him prisoner in the basement.

He wondered where Jack and his father were. Almost immediately, Mrs Pickering answered the question for him.

"The others," she said, "are in with *him.* With Mr Blagger. Jack'll go out and fetch us some chips later. I've got more to do than cooking."

"Sorting?" suggested Ned cunningly. It worked.

"Sorting!" she cried. "A heap of it – and half of it for keeping, from what I see. You come along, and let's have a look at it!

"You see, dear," she confided, "you got to keep your feet on the ground, in a case like this. Mr Pickering, he don't think this worth the while – no need of it, he says, with treasure round the corner. But what I say is that there's birds in the hand and there's birds in the bush, and this" – she waved towards the heap – "is birds in the *hand.*"

They both stood staring at it.

"I shall have to begin!" she cried suddenly, and dived in – straight to the green crocheted jumper she had showed him earlier. "And this!" She swooped again, and came up with a chipped enamel saucepan. These she set down nearby, then turned again to the pile.

"What shall I do?" asked Ned. "I don't really know which things you want and which you don't."

"What you do, is sort under headings, see," she told him. "You put toys together, and crocks, and electric, and clothes and suchlike. You put 'em all in piles, and I'll go round after and skim off the pickings."

Half an hour later there was barely a square yard of floor space left in the room. The pile of jumble had become twenty little piles – of which by far the largest was Mrs Pickering's own hoard of "pickings".

She sank down into a chair, all at once deflated, the excitement over.

"That's that, then," she observed. "You've done very well, for a beginner, though I see you've mixed clothes and soft furnishings."

Ned went over and began to throw cushions and curtains into a separate pile.

"Never mind," she said to herself, "there'll be more tomorrow. I'll put the kettle on."

As she spoke, the other two came in. At the first horrified glance Ned could see that Jack's black eye certainly *looked* as if it had been meant. At present it was not entirely a *black* eye – more a green, yellow and purple eye. In Jack's white face it was horrible – it looked almost bad enough to *die* of.

Ned stood speechless. At that moment, it did not seem possible that Jack and he could contrive ever again to live under the same roof, let alone speak to one another. Mrs Pickering's next remark did nothing to improve matters.

"Jack!" she shrieked. "Just look at it! It'll drop out – I swear it will!"

Jack, alarmed, clapped up a hand to his eye, hit the bruise and let out a yell of his own.

"Less said about that the better," said Mr Pickering, and the look he gave Ned was like the one Mrs Pickering had given him earlier – almost as if seeing him again in a new light, or even seeing him for the first time.

"Where's my nails, Mother, and the hammer?" he went on. "Where's all my tools, in fact?"

"They're under our bed," she returned, "in that box, as you'd know full well if you'd get down there as I've asked you a dozen times and put that loose castor back on. Might as well be at sea, the way that bed rocks. What do you want 'em for?"

Ned by now could recognise easily one of the glances that flashed from Pickering to Pickering when there were things to be kept secret from himself.

"I'll get 'em," was all Mr Pickering said, having flashed one of those certain glances. "And Jack can go off for the supper."

"My eye hurts," whined Jack.

"I'll fetch them," offered Ned eagerly, glad of the chance of escaping from the basement even for a few minutes, and at the same time making some kind of recompense for that awful eye.

"Go on, then," said Mrs Pickering. "You go. Not that it takes an *eye* to walk a few yards down the road."

Ned, picturing what his own mother's reactions would be to an eye of that appearance, was shocked despite himself. Mr Pickering went out, followed by Jack, and Mrs Pickering produced a carrier bag and a purse.

"You'd best get cod and chips for four," she told him, "and plaice for *him*."

When Ned returned, supper was laid out ready in the scullery but still there was no sign of Jack or Mr Pickering.

"Give them here," she said, "I'll put 'em out, and you can take Mr Blagger's tray and tell the others their suppers is ready."

Standing outside Mr Blagger's door, performing his usual manoeuvre with the tray to make knocking possible, Ned felt thankful that Mr Blagger would not be alone.

"Who is it?" came Mr Pickering's voice.

"It's me. I've brought Mr Blagger's supper. And yours is on the table."

"Wait a minute."

What Ned had to wait seemed very much longer than a minute, and he could hear scuffling, banging, whispering voices. When the door did open, it was half Jack's face and the horrific eye that appeared and Ned nearly dropped the tray. The door opened a little wider, but still not far enough for Ned to see into the room beyond.

"Here, give it me." Ned passed over the tray. "And tell ma we're coming."

The door shut. Whatever, *whatever* was going on behind it?

Back in the scullery Mrs Pickering was already

well into her cod and chips and Ned, seating himself, followed suit. It was the best meal he had had since he left home.

"Good idea, this," he said, and added hastily, "Saves you a lot of work."

"Not same as home cooking, of course," she observed through a mouthful of chips, and Ned silently agreed that it was not – not in this particular home, at any rate.

Mr Pickering and Jack appeared, ate their supper, and returned to Mr Blagger's room. Whatever it was they were doing in there, judging by the hammering and knocking and banging, it was not playing patience. Ned did the washing up for Mrs Pickering, and then went into the living-room where she was having a final picking over of the day's takings.

"I think I'll have an early night," he told her.

"Yes, you get off, then," she said absently. "Sea air. *This* might do, if it was taken up a bit. Wouldn't go with the green, of course." She was holding up a pink satin skirt.

"Oh, I don't *know*," and she tossed it into the pile of "keepings".

In the bedroom Ned changed into his pyjamas, chose a book, found his notepaper and pen, then climbed into bed. If Jack came in, he would slip the paper into the book and pretend to be reading.

"I'll probably know when he's coming," he thought. "When that row stops."

The banging from Mr Blagger's room was louder than ever here, almost directly opposite, and was all the more mysterious because Mr Blagger did not seem at all the sort of man who would go in for banging and hammering.

"P'raps it's the Pickerings who are hammering," he thought, "while *he* plays patience."

He took a sheet of notepaper and tried to concentrate. He had already decided what he was going to say – he had decided it on the long walk from the Dallakers' bay to the pullover that afternoon.

"Dear Mother," he wrote, "Thank you very much for your letter. I'm glad you and Duke are missing me – I'm missing you as well." As he wrote, in that cold room under the harsh glare of the naked bulb, this became suddenly unbearably true. "As a matter of fact, I'm feeling really homesick, and I think I'd like to come home before the end of the holidays. It's not that I don't like it here, it's just that I want to come home. So please can I, next week? I don't think the Pickerings will be annoyed because

Mrs Pickering can see that I'm off my food." (This, he felt, was a good touch.) "I will ring you up in a day or two to say when I will be coming. The wind is very cold here" (another good touch) "though it hasn't rained much. If I get a cold, they won't be surprised if I want to go home. I'm really looking forward to seeing you and Duke again. Lots of love, Ned."

He re-read the letter, and was satisfied. This was his escape route. Today was Saturday, so if he posted it tomorrow she would not receive it till after the weekend and there would be no danger of her coming down herself to see how he was. But once the treasure was found and the Dallakers had set sail, to go on staying with the Pickerings would be impossible. He had not bothered to unpack his suitcase – for that matter, no one had suggested that he should, and so far as he could see, there was nowhere to put things in any case.

He put the letter in an envelope, addressed it, and placed it under his pillow. Then he got out of bed, turned off the light and groped his way back. By the time he was actually in bed he could see quite well again by the light of the street lamp through the uncurtained window. The sodium made all things not light but mud. "This could be how it seems to a frog," he thought, "at the bottom of a pond," and he stared about the room with his new frog eyes.

The sound of hammering had stopped now. Ned's thoughts turned back to the Dallakers, out there on the windy, darkened beach, waiting for the night tide. He pictured the blown seaweed rising and flying in the moonlight, the phosphorescence out beyond the bay. He remembered Fiony's words, "If you want to see her, you will – even if you're asleep."

Perhaps it really did work. If you banged your head on the pillow six times before you went to sleep, you woke up at six o'clock – that was what people said. It worked, too – or at least it had the only time he had tried it. But how many times did you bang your head on the pillow to catch a tide with treasure on it?

He lay picturing the *Sea Queen*, fiercely, first her curving shape, her masts, prow, then the details – coiled ropes, wet and sea-stained, barnacles brown grey white and speckled – even the smell of her – tar, twine, salt, timber . . .

He woke suddenly. It was still dark. He shot upright in bed. Was it now . . .? Again the *Sea Queen* rose before him in uncanny detail. Then he heard noises in the corridor outside, stealthy footsteps and wheels – *wheels*? – rolling over the uncarpeted floor. He looked at the luminous dial of his watch. Three o'clock. Jack lay snoring gently in the bed opposite. Now something heavy was being dragged up the basement stairs. Overhead came slow footsteps. They stopped.

"At the front door," he thought. He strained his ears, but heard no sound of the door either opening or closing. After a minute or so he lay back again, but still he listened.

Now there were more sounds – outside, this time. Ned leapt out of bed and went to the window, craning up.

Between the iron railings he saw a pair of trousered legs. Behind, drawn by rope, appeared what looked like a low trolley on wheels – the kind that he and his friends had often made for joyriding – go-carts.

The legs, without doubt, belonged to Mr Blagger. There was no doubt, either, where he was going. He was going to the beach, to walk the tide line among the flying weed. And he was taking the trolley to carry a brass-bound chest – a chest too heavy, perhaps, to carry single-handed.

"I'm going after him," Ned decided. "It's tonight!"

He turned sharply from the window. His foot struck something hard, he put out a hand to steady himself and there was a resounding clatter. A chair! Jack gave a kind of surprised snort and the sound of his breathing stopped. Ned, breath held, ducked and crawled swiftly on to his own bed from the foot, pulling the cover over him.

"Hey!" He heard Jack's whisper. "You awake?"

Ned forced himself to breathe slowly. He heard springs creak, feet pattering on the lino, another clatter as Jack's foot struck the fallen chair, and a stifled yell of pain.

Then he felt Jack's presence by his bedside, even through closed lids he knew that he was there. In . . . out . . . in . . . out . . . Ned had feigned sleep a hundred times before when his mother had tiptoed into his room.

"Hey!" he heard Jack whisper again.

In . . . out . . . in . . . out . . . The footsteps pattered away again. Still Ned breathed in a slow, even rhythm. He dared not stop. In . . . out . . . in . . . out . . .

He breathed himself into sleep.

Chapter 12

The Pickerings had a secret. Ned sensed it within half an hour of waking. It was to do, he knew, with wheels in the night. The Scavengers were cock-a-hoop. Never before had the air been so thick with darting glances – even Jack's eye, slitted under its puffing purple, managed them.

"You take the tray along, dear," cried Mrs Pickering, and they watched him, all three, as he lifted it carefully and carried it out.

"Come in!" came Mr Blagger's voice almost immediately. "Come in, boy!"

He was seated at the table. It was as if he had not moved since Ned had last seen him. He was playing patience, or reading the cards, as a fortune-teller does.

"Put it down," he ordered. "And wait."

Ned placed the tray on another, smaller table by the grate and stood waiting, looking about the room. It was littered with wood shavings, nails, screws.

"That's what they were doing last night," he thought. "Making the trolley."

By the door was a pair of wellington boots. There was sand on them. His eyes moved rapidly about the room, looking for clues.

Then he saw it. He let out an audible gasp of dismay.

Mr Blagger turned slowly in his chair and Ned jerked his eyes away from it, forced himself to meet Mr Blagger's gaze and summoned all his newly-found powers of acting to appear casual and unconcerned.

"Yes, boy?"

Ned stared. He had seen very little of the *face.* Mr Blagger spent all his life in holes underground. His face was white, his eyes were curiously short-sighted-looking.

"I thought you spoke."

"N – no. I was just waiting, like you said."

"I have forgotten," said Mr Blagger, "why I told you to wait. I daresay there was a reason, but I have forgotten it. I daresay you sometimes forget things yourself?"

The last words were spoken heavily, with meaning. He knew.

"Yes – well, I do, sometimes," Ned said.

"A pity. You remember, no doubt, your instructions?"

"Yes. Oh yes, sir."

"Forget them."

"F – forget?"

"Everything." Mr Blagger's face, incapable of looking pleased, looked – satisfied. Then slowly, almost as if painfully, he turned in his chair and Ned was left looking at the back of his head again.

"Yes. Yes. All right, I'll forget. I'll remember. I mean–"

Ned made for the door. Outside, his instinct was to make for the stairs, straight out of the house and down to the bay. He hesitated by the foot of the stairs, then went back through the littered living-room and into the scullery.

The three Pickerings looked up as he entered, but he took his place at the table and picked up his spoon, all the time saying to himself over and over again, "They mustn't know that I know. They mustn't know that I know."

"Shan't do any Knocking today," announced Mr Pickering. "Stop in and do a bit of glueing. Might as well get rid of what we've got."

"And you'll be going to the beach, dear, shan't you?" cried Mrs Pickering.

"Yes! Yes – I will!"

The wind had strengthened in the night and was blowing in from the sea, a *heathen* wind, noisy and biting, beating its way through the town. When he reached the pullover it met him head on, pushing him with a rudeness that was almost personal – made him feel like pushing back. Sand and seaweed flew about him as he lowered his head and struck out towards the distant dunes. Each time he lifted his head and stared into the stinging sand they seemed as far away as ever. "I'll never get there," he even found himself thinking.

The sea itself was grey and towering, coming in savagely, like a marauder.

"They must be there. They *must*," Ned told himself, but he did not believe it. He believed that when at last he mounted the dunes and looked down into the bay, it would be empty.

The tide was still on the ebb and the *Sea Queen* lay shining in the wind and light on the blinding puddles of the flats. White gulls carved the air in huge arcs, making the patterns of the wind.

There was no sign of the Dallakers, but Ned shouted as he ran – "Ahoy! Ahoy!" – because the shout was a relief, not a greeting. The wind caught his voice and tossed it skyward to the screaming gulls.

He did not wait for an invitation to come aboard. Spurting sand he raced by the stern to where the ladder dangled and seized the damp rope.

"Ahoy!" he shouted again as he climbed, and as he drew level with the deck saw Fiony and her father by the companion-way. With a final effort he heaved himself aboard and gasped out his news with the little breath he had left.

"They've – got – it! I've seen it! Oh, they've got it!"

Battered by wind and the glaring sea light he saw their stares of disbelief and for an instant doubted the witness of his own eyes. That marvellous chest could not have come aground at last in the Pickerings' dark basement, could not have fallen into the hands of Scavengers.

Mr Dallaker advanced slowly.

"What was that?" he said. "What was that again?"

Ned blurted out his story, knowing how

impossible it seemed to the listening Dallakers. They had not visited the cold basement, smelled its smells, watched the thick white dealing fingers.

"There was a cloth over it," he finished, "but I saw it – just the end of it. And there was brass, just like you said, a sort of handle."

The gulls wheeled indifferently, the waves rose and fell, the Dallakers stared at him with disbelief. Was it true?

"No!" Fiony screamed suddenly. "No, no, *no*!"

She burst into tears and turned her back and ran to the prow, facing out to sea while the wind whipped up her hair and skirts.

Ned groaned.

"Oh crikey. I'm *sorry*. If only I hadn't kicked that chair over! I could've come and told you, and–"

He broke off. Mr Dallaker was not listening.

"T'ain't true," he said slowly. "I don't believe *that*."

"But I saw it!"

"Captain'll know it ain't true."

"You could get it back again. Tonight, when they're asleep! I could let you in. I know where it is–"

"Not after all these years beachcombing.

Treasure's not for Scavengers. Treasure's not that easy to come by. It's for them that watches, and works, and waits."

The Captain appeared.

"Morning!" He shouted the word distinctly into the racketing wind.

"Tell him," said Mr Dallaker. "Tell him what you told me."

Ned told him, but on this second telling the story seemed oddly less true even to himself – more like a description of what he had seen in a play or film than something that had actually happened. The *Sea Queen* and the Dallakers were working their usual magic, making mere shadows of the Scavengers and their littered world. Fiony, her face tear-stained, came slowly from the prow to listen.

At the end the Captain shook his head slowly.

"Don't know what you saw down there, boy. But it wasn't treasure."

"Wasn't?"

"Grandpa!" Fiony flung her arms about him. "I knew! I knew!"

"But I saw it! I saw it!"

"Makes no matter what you saw," returned the Captain calmly. "That treasure's still afloat and still to come."

"But how do you know? He was down here in the night – I heard him go. They made a trolley to carry it back. And *I saw it.*"

It seemed that the only way he could go on believing his own eyes was to keep on saying it, over and over again. "I saw it."

"*Something* you saw," agreed the Captain.

"But was it something you was *meant* to see?" said Mr Dallaker suddenly. "Not like Scavengers to leave treasure lying about to be seen by them that isn't *meant* to see. In particular not like the Chief Scavenger."

Ned stared. Meaning dawned.

"That's it! He told me to wait – and that was when I saw it – and saw his boots with the sand on. Then he pretended he didn't know why he'd asked me to wait. That's it! He meant me to see!"

"And to come and tell us!" Fiony's face was pink again. "So we'd go away!"

"Which we shan't," said Mr Dallaker grimly. "Not till that brass-bound box is safely stowed below, where it belongs. Come hell," he added, "or high water."

"Or both," though Ned. He could see the looming grey rollers beyond, and thought of the circling Scavengers.

"Better not look too pleased," he said. "Jack'll

be in those dunes, watching, sure as anything. Better try and look tragic, or something."

The Captain began to shake his head. Mr Dallaker clapped a hand to his brow and Fiony fetched out a handkerchief and dashed it fiercely into her eyes.

"I hope I do it better than that," Ned thought. "Still – from a distance – and through one eye . . ."

"We got to be careful," Mr Dallaker said. "They're playing a queer game."

"They don't trust me, or they wouldn't have gone to all that trouble over the chest. They knew I was really on your side, and I'd come straight down here and tell you. Jack must've heard us, Fiony, yesterday."

"Must've." Her voice was muffled by the handkerchief.

"What you better do," said Mr Dallaker thoughtfully, "is go back and act miserable. And don't say a word unless they ask you."

"Which they will."

"When they *do*, don't you still say a word about seeing that made-up chest. I got a plan coming."

The rest of them stood silent, watching him, waiting for the plan to come.

"What we don't want," he murmured, "is them Scavengers down on this beach tonight."

"High tide 5.20," put in the Captain, and his stoical face lit up so that it was for a moment unrecognisable. It was lucky he had his back to the dunes, thought Ned, and Jack's watchful eye.

"You mean you're really sure it's going to be then? How can you be, after all these years?"

"It's only on *account* of all these years," replied Mr Dallaker, "that we *do* know. No good us trying to explain to you, lad, with respect. No offence. You got your world nailed, I daresay, and we got ours. So far as is possible, that is," he added.

"Some ways, we're playing the same game, them and us." The Captain sounded thoughtful.

"They got a spy, *we* got a spy," agreed Mr Dallaker. "Same one, even."

"They got a treasure chest . . ." prompted the Captain.

"And *we've* got one!"

All the three other Dallakers spoke in unison, so loudly and joyfully that Ned glanced swiftly back over his shoulder in the direction of the dunes.

"*You* have?" he himself spoke in a hoarse

whisper, hoping to bring their voices down to match.

"And a real one! Twin of the lost 'un. Brass-bound twin!"

"And they mean us to think *they've* the treasure," Fiony cried, "and we can make 'em believe the same thing!"

"Use the chest as decoy," said the Captain. "Draw them off while we get the real 'un!"

"Careful," said Mrs Dallaker. "We must be careful. Make sure it all fits. We should lose the chest, Matthew."

"That one, aye! But to get its brass-bound twin – *that*'s fair exchange, Nell!"

"Oh and Mother, we shall be a-sail again tomorrow, and there'll be pearls and rubies and gold and silver and it'll be all our dreams come true! What's an empty old chest beside all that? I *long* to see a ruby, Mother, and a real pearl!"

"Come, lass," Mr Dallaker put an arm. Across her thin, shawled shoulders. "You'll give up an empty chest for a ruby, won't you? Or is it more than that even you want?"

"Oh you know it's not!" she burst out. "Such nonsense! Me in pearls! It's them thieving Scavengers. I don't want to see 'em reaping *anything* – not an empty box, even, not so much as a brass nail belonging to us. But if it can't be done, it can't, and we shall have to let it go."

"Unless we have it out straight," he said.

"Straight? You mean–?"

"Them and us. Tonight. Best to win."

"O Father – no!"

"Don't know but what it wouldn't be better. Scavengers is the best to deceive – always has been. That's their game, and them more likely to beat us at it. Make 'em play *our* game!"

"But in the dark, Father, and Scavengers all round! I'm scared to do it! Let's use the chest! Let's!"

"That's their game," he repeated. "We'll play ours. Tell you what" – a lightness spread over his face then – not quite a smile, but the dawning of one. "Let's be open and above-board and catch 'em in their own trap!"

Mrs Dallaker was frowning, her long brown fingers plucking at the fringes of her shawl.

"I don't know what you mean, Matthew," she said.

"Let 'em make their *own* traps, and fall right into 'em!" he cried triumphantly. "That's it! I got it now!"

"Still don't know what you're talking about," she said.

"Oh, you will! Oh, it's easy!"

Ned felt lightness spreading over himself, too, without in the least knowing why. He felt light, as if he could fly.

"You go back," Mr Dallaker told him, "and you tell 'em all they want to know. You answer every single question they ask you, and you answer it true."

"True? Give it all away?" The lightness fled in an instant.

"Give it away. You tell the Scavengers the truth. Only thing that'll fox 'em now – the truth."

The wind buffeted between them and Ned's eyes, staring hard into it, ran water.

"Oh Mr Dallaker," he cried, "you don't know! You just don't know!"

And behind the cry came unspoken words and pictures of pattering hands, sharp eyes, thick white dealing fingers. Mr Blagger, rooted in his dark basement, moveless but for the deliberate hands, was dealing destruction.

"I know Scavengers," came the reply.

"But Mr Blagger! Do you know *him*?"

The Scavengers were human, recognisable. But not so the big man whom Ned knew chiefly as a broad back, as a silhouette against the light that shone down on the green velvet cloth and the cards and fingers.

"Never met him face to face," Mr Dallaker admitted. "But I can guess. He's a Scavenger, ain't he? And human?"

"No! No! He's not human! He's . . . he's . . ."

But because he could not finish, because he had not the least idea what Mr Blagger was, and because he despaired of ever communicating to the Dallakers the awfulness of Mr Blagger's set back and head, of his absolute absorption and stillness, he said nothing at all. He stared through the cold wind at the thin, urgent faces of the Dallakers and silently willed them, despite everything, to succeed, to win back to the sea with their treasure.

"You'll come back? This afternoon? Tell us what they say?"

He nodded. It crossed his mind that someone in the dunes saw the nod, was guessing at its meaning.

"We're *all* in the dark," he thought.

Chapter 13

Two hours later Ned went back to town on Jack's invisible heels. The streets were nearly empty, swept clean by the wind.

"This is a ghost town," he thought, and meant it. Nothing about it seemed real except the wind, so strong now that it blotted out everything else. The world was reduced to a pure, vast rush of deafening air. He could not even *think* for wind.

The door of Number Eleven Bakers Road shut behind him and in the instant the wind went. There was sudden quiet. He felt his senses – sight, touch, smell – returning. The world was back with him again, and for a moment he was dizzy with the shock of it.

Steamy odours mixed with the strong, fish

smell of glue met him as he entered the dim living-room, still littered with the sorted heaps of Miscellaneous. He guessed that the Pickerings were in the scullery. He pushed open the door and saw them seated with their elbows on the oilcloth, waiting for him. He felt their eyes raking him for clues and signs. He almost panicked. Then he remembered.

"It doesn't *matter*," he told himself. "You're not acting any more. You can't give anything away. You're going to tell them the *truth*."

And if they read the truth in his face as well as heard it from his lips, so much the better. He forced himself to meet their gaze.

"Well, dear!" said Mrs Pickering at last. "You *do* look pasty about the face. You sit down, and I'll get your dinner."

Ned went to his chair but Mrs Pickering showed no sign of moving.

"Been down on the beach, have you?" she enquired.

He nodded.

"Anything to tell us, dear?" she continued. "To report?"

Again he nodded.

"Oh, yes?" She spoke the words encouragingly, enquiringly.

Ned licked his dry lips. Part of him knew that he must do as Mr Dallaker had told him. The other (and by far the stronger) part was crying silently "Beware!" The words that he had to say were almost impossible, but he said them.

"It's tonight!"

It was done. His voice sounded hoarse and unreal. He cleared his throat and said it again, "It's tonight!" and recognised the voice as his own this time.

The three Pickerings sat alert, intent. Ned went on: "High tide's at 5.20. That's when it'll come."

They still watched.

"The chest, I mean," he added lamely, sensing that he was not nearly as convincing now that he was telling the truth as he had been before when he was acting – or lying.

The faces of the Scavengers were blank and bare of any kind of feeling – surprise, delight, triumph. They were simply concentrated into this intentness, this waiting stillness.

"It's true!" Ned cried, almost scared by their reluctance to be moved. "They told me! The Captain *knows* it'll be tonight! And they're going out with the treasure on the ebb tide – they told me that, as well!"

Still no flicker of response.

"It's *true*!" he cried again.

"Oh yes, dear," said Mrs Pickering then – soothingly, as if humouring him. "Of course it is. You've done very well, hasn't he, Arthur?"

"My word, he has!" Ned was startled by the unaccustomed heartiness of Mr Pickering's voice, by the exaggerated rubbing together of his thin hands.

"*He's* acting!" he thought incredulously. "They're pretending to believe me, but they don't!"

"I'll get the dinner now, dears," said Mrs Pickering, and got up. The other three sat silent while she banged merrily at the stove, talking in snatches under her breath. "*There* we are! Now what did I do . . .? The whisk, where's the . . .? Oooops-a-daisy!"

"As if nothing had happened," Ned thought. Then, "If they don't believe it, they won't go down to the beach at dawn."

Then, at last, with a slow, marvellous blaze of understanding: "Exactly like Mr Dallaker planned! I told them the truth, and they didn't believe it! They can't believe anyone would actually tell the truth! They've fallen right into the trap! It worked!"

"Jack'll take Mr Blagger's tray today," said Mrs Pickering. "Won't you, Jack?"

"And tell him what I said," Ned thought. "And *he* won't believe it, either!"

His exultation rushed up into his throat. He wanted to jump up, shout, sing! He gripped his hands tightly together under the table and tried to order his face.

"Crikey, crikey, crikey . . ." his own voice ran in his head. It was not enough. He must say something out loud. Elaborate on his triumph.

"So it'll be easy for you," he said. "Just get down there early, and–" he left the sentence in mid-air.

"Oooh, easy as wink!" agreed Mrs Pickering almost absently, ladling gravy. "Up, up, up in the world, and all as easy as wink!"

Ned noticed she was wearing the lime-green crocheted jumper, and realised that this perhaps accounted for her gaiety. She caught his look.

"Like it? Lovely shade. And there's something so ladylike and a bit tasteful about crochet, I always think."

She tucked in her chin and peered down at it, the saucepan, forgotten, tilting dangerously in her hand.

"The gravy, Mother," warned Mr Pickering,

and Ned, looking from one to the other of them, tried again to see them as villains, and failed. He saw them as grubby, greedy – and human.

Only Mr Blagger, still as stone but for the slowly dealing hands, moveless in his small back room, seemed like a threat. Mr Blagger was faceless – or nearly so. He was The Enemy.

"It looks very nice," said Ned then, to save the gravy, and Mrs Pickering tossed her head like a duchess and drawing her overall tightly over the jumper with one hand, swoopingly poured gravy with the other. It seemed a shame, Ned thought, that she was *not* to go up in the world. She had obviously rehearsed for it so long.

He pushed the thought away.

"They *are* The Enemy," he told himself fiercely. He deliberately tried to picture the shore in the darkness, just before dawn. He conjured up the terror of a darkness surely thronged with invisible enemies. He saw clearly how the roar of wind and waves would drown the sounds of pursuit – even the screams and cries of capture. With an effort he saw Mr Blagger himself down there – faceless still, but striding.

A plate was put down before him and with a shock he came to. He was dizzy, poised again between the two worlds – Pickering Dallaker

Pickering Dallaker Pickering . . . But the dark and spray and thunder of the beach vanished and left real a plate of steaming stew. And at that moment he even welcomed the realness of the Pickerings' scullery, and their stained oilskin cloth and the savoury steam. (That, above all, was real.) He picked up his knife and fork and let the picture of the dark beach go.

"Mr Blagger," said Mrs Pickering.

Jack got up and took the tray. He went out.

"Keeps himself to himself," remarked Mrs Pickering, seating herself. "You'll've noticed, dear?"

"Mr Blagger?" Ned asked. "Or Jack?"

"Just listen!" she cried. "Sharp as a thorn! Jack indeed! No dear. Jack's a quiet boy, we see that. But not standoffish. Oh no. Is he, Arthur? Not a bit standoffish?"

Mr Pickering denied through a mouthful of vegetables that Jack was in any way off standing – or standoffish.

"It's being an only," said Mrs Pickering confidingly. "We've always thought that, haven't we, Arthur?"

Her husband again made the right noises of agreement, muffled this time by a great bite of bread he had just taken.

"Now them *Beachcombers*," she went on, "*they're* stuck up, if you like. Heads in the clouds, noses in the air, that's what we've always said. Neither rhyme nor reason in them, not that *we* can see. And to hear their opinions of dry land – you'd think it was dirt, the way they go on!"

It occurred to Ned that so it was, literally speaking, but he did not say so.

"Anyhow, we're glad *we're* out of it," she went on smugly. "Safe and sound on dry land, with a roof over our heads. Aren't we, Arthur?"

He swallowed hard.

"No money in it," he said thickly.

"That's just it!" she cried. "No more there is! Not a penny, so far as we can see. And what a way to bring up children!"

Ned silently compared Jack with Fiony. He opened his mouth to begin to explain to her what he thought the rewards of a Beachcomber's life might be – money apart, of course. But he closed it again almost immediately. The eager bent of a ship's prow, the cold water smells by the sea's edge, the wind, sky and sea fusing into a new and miraculous element of beauty and adventure – the words that said what he really meant about all these things would not form, here in the Pickerings' dark and littered basement. He could not bring the two worlds together here, any more than he could ever explain to the Dallakers the strange power of those dealing hands or the sly greed of the Pickerings.

"There's one thing," she said comfortably, stroking her green jumper. "There's a sight more Scavengers than there is Beachcombers, if it comes to a showdown. People isn't silly. Soon as they see there's nothing to be got by beachcombing, they get ashore where they know what's what. It's a great thing, you know" – she made to pat Ned's hand, but missed – "a great thing, to know what's what."

"I'm sure it is," he agreed quickly.

"And that's just what them Beachcombers never know. If you was to ask me, they're about done. What they call a dying race."

"Oh no!" cried Ned. But he cried silently.

"And once we've our hands on that treasure, Mother" – Mr Pickering was wiping his mouth on the back of his hand – "dead and done."

"No," said Ned grimly. "No." It was as if the protest were all the stronger for being a silent one – as if words unspoken had more power than those said aloud.

Jack came back into the scullery. The others had all finished. He sat down and began shovelling food into his mouth as if making up for lost time.

Mrs Pickering watched him almost fondly.

"Not a bad lad," she murmured. "Get him some new clothes, eh, Arthur, and smarten him up. Make a new lad of him."

She evidently had great faith in the power of clothes. And having seen with his own eyes the effect of the lime crocheted jumper on her own behaviour (when she remembered she was wearing it, that is) Ned was almost inclined to think she might be right.

"And yet," she spoke absently, half to herself, "I've said it before, and I'll say it again. I shall *miss* all this when we've gone up in the world. I sometimes wonder what we shall *do* all day."

"Nothing," said Mr Pickering. "Live like lords."

"Mmmmm." She got up and began stacking the plates. "*Is* that what lords do, Arthur? Nothing, I mean."

"Course it is. Make haste, Jack, and we'll get this lot glued and cleared out. Shan't want a room full of stuff left behind when we're ready for the getaway."

So the Scavengers, too, were planning a getaway. Ned saw another cue, and took it.

"It'll be tomorrow, won't it? The getaway, I mean?"

The Pickerings exchanged glances. An unpleasant smile flickered over Jack's face.

"That's right," agreed Mr Pickering. "Tomorrow. Soon's we get our hands on that treasure."

"He wants to see him." It was Jack speaking. Ned knew at once what he meant. His heart hammered.

"Will it do when I get back? I was going to get down to the beach and see if I can find out any more about – you know . . ."

Mrs Pickering was slowly shaking her head. There was no choice. Standing in the narrow passage and summoning up courage to knock, Ned found that he was trembling. His knees felt actually weak, as they did after a spell of illness in bed. He knocked.

Silence. He waited, then knocked again.

"Come in."

He went in and closed the door behind him. He did not advance further into the room, but stood staring across it at the outline of Mr Blagger's head and shoulders against the light shafting down from the high, barred window. There was no sound but for the ticking of a big metal alarum clock on the shelf and the soft slither of the playing cards.

Ned cleared his throat.

"Er – they said you wanted to see me. Sir," he said.

There was no reply. Ned waited. He fixed his eyes on the back of Mr Blagger's head, willing him to turn round – speak – anything to break that slow silence. It seemed as if a full five minutes passed.

Still Ned stood. There was nothing really to prevent his going, he knew. But it was as if he were chained there, fixed hand and foot, hypnotised by his own fear and by the loud ticking of the clock. It rang like iron in the silence and struck against the walls of the room.

"I'll wait two more minutes, then I'll go," he thought. But he knew that he would not. If his fear were to fade, if the clock stopped, only then would he be released.

"I'll think of something else," he thought. "I'll think about the Dallakers and the *Sea Queen.*"

He tried. He even closed his eyes to let the pictures form against the lids as he did just before sleep. Nothing came. He clenched his fists and squeezed his eyes and willed the *Sea Queen* to take shape, but the harder he tried the harder his heart beat and the more insistent became the ticking of the clock. He could summon nothing – neither the Beachcombers nor the *Sea Queen* nor even a picture of the sea itself. It was as if he were held in a spell and the spell was to do with darkness and to do with Mr Blagger and the turning of the cards and the relentless clock, and the spell was a spell that stopped all movement dead in its flight, that held everything frozen, powerless to move. It was as though life itself were trapped as if by the shutter of a camera, the whole world reduced to a negative.

And he tried to turn towards the door but he could not and he tried even to *imagine* going through that door and up those darkened stairs and out into the air and daylight and down to the beach and the lift and fall of waves and great rushing curves of wind and air. He could not.

But in the midst of his panic he said to himself quite clearly and firmly as if to a very young child: "I may not be able to see the Beachcombers, but I know they are real. They're still there, *and* the *Sea Queen.* I know it."

It was almost like a prayer. And just then Mr Blagger spoke. He said one word only: "Go!"

And he did not even turn his head to say it.

Chapter 14

It took nearly all Ned's pocket-money to buy the alarm clock. When the assistant told him the price he did not even hesitate. He was buying more than just a clock, he knew that.

"If I had any faith," he told himself as he put his shoulder sideways to the wind, "if I had any *faith*, I wouldn't've needed to buy it. Fiony said I'd wake anyway. Want to wake and you will, she said."

With the clock in his pocket and his own part in the dawn adventure certain now, he felt a new excitement. He turned right into the wind, swallowed it in bucketfuls, and as he breasted the pullover felt sure that a day like this was worth a thousand other, ordinary days. The sky was grey and so was the sea and he thought that probably even the *wind* must be grey, but he shouted aloud as he raced down the slope and threw out his arms to embrace it.

He had won a victory over the Pickerings, had escaped unharmed from Mr Blagger's petrifying spell.

"Would I have turned to *stone* if I'd stayed?" he wondered. "It felt like it."

When he mounted the ridge of dunes and looked down into the blindingly wet and gleaming bay he saw the Dallakers in a little group, beards and hair streaming, their bones shining through their wind-flattened rags, being *played* on.

"Jubilee!" he said, under his breath. "Oh Jubilee!"

And he went down and joined them and they stood silent while he told them how the Pickerings had refused to believe the truth, and how Mr Blagger had almost turned him to stone in that small back room. But even as he told it, even as he tried to find the right words to explain that awful silence and movelessness, that certainty that he was rooted, could stir neither hand nor foot, even as he told it, the wind was there contradicting him. It racketed among them, tugging, swooping, *shouting*, and Ned, staring into the Dallakers' thin faces, gave up.

"It's no good. I can't make you understand how it was. I never could, not in a thousand years. And I don't even believe it myself now – here – except I *know* it happened."

"But you got away," said Mr Dallaker.

"Yes." He looked back at their grave, listening faces, and said no more. Pickering Dallaker Pickering Dallaker Pickering Dallaker – the pendulum swung and stopped.

"For ever," Ned thought. "This time, forever. Whatever happens now."

And he grinned joyfully at them and their faces too lightened as if they read his thoughts. The others turned to the task of making ready the *Sea Queen* while Fiony and Ned wandered off along the shore alone.

"I wonder," said Fiony softly. "I wonder, I wonder, I wonder . . ."

"What? What do you wonder?"

"About you." She stopped and faced him. "Where you belong."

"On land, I suppose."

"But not with Scavengers, Ned – never could be."

Ned kept his eyes fixed on reflections in the

wet sand by the sea's edge, flat and calm despite the wind's fury.

"And you know what I wish?" she went on, and bent her head, too, to stare at the sand. "You know what I wish and *wish*–?"

"No." But in the same moment he knew what she would say.

"That you'd come."

Afterword

And now you know what the snag was. That is where it ends, just like that: "That you'd come."

It was only the last few pages that were spoilt, only three of them, written both sides, but enough to leave the final mystery unsolved. These pages look as if they have been wet at some time and then dried out, or bleached, perhaps, by the sun. They were the outer leaves of the bundle.

I even took them to a forensic laboratory. They were very helpful (I had to invent a story – make out the papers might be connected with some crime) but even they could make out only the odd word here and there. Everyone keeps talking about how marvellous modern technology is, but when you want to know something really important, it lets you down.

At the end I was left where I had started – at a dead end (or at the very beginning) with the words:

"That you'd come."

The nights I have spent, tossing and sleepless, trying to get to the truth of the thing. Because if I knew the truth, for *certain*, then I could write the ending myself (using a kind of poetic licence). The trouble is that, far from knowing what *Ned* would have done, I can't even decide for certain what *I'd* have done in exactly the same circumstances.

There were really only two choices. I have the feeling that Ned could not have compromised, could not have said "I'll come with you just for a fortnight", and then come ashore again and gone home. In fact, I have a strong feeling that after even a day at sea with the Beachcombers, out of sight of land, Ned would have stayed forever. I think that the Dallakers were people of magic, faeries. At first I was not sure, but as I look at the last few chapters of the manuscript the hints and clues seem stronger and clearer until at last he sees their bones "shining through their wind-flattened rags". If Ned had gone with them he might even have lost his memory, as Rip van Winkle did, lost all sense of hours, days, years – been at sea in time, as well as in space.

How could he have decided to go, I ask myself – left his mother, home, friends, cast anchor and left the whole world behind? But then I ask myself, how could he have stayed? How gone down to that empty beach before dawn and watched the Beachcombers sail into the breaking sky with their treasure? How gone back to that basement and the Pickerings and Mr Blagger? It is unimaginable.

It has even occurred to me that perhaps there *was* no treasure that April morning, that the North Sea rollers came in high and bitter and grey and the wind behind them blew only a drizzle of cold salt over the beach and the town beyond where the people were sleeping still behind their drawn curtains.

Oddly, the question of the treasure itself teases me hardly at all. It is Ned's decision that seems important to me – go or stay? In the littered world of the Pickerings (which I suppose is the world most of us know, in a way) at least, as Mrs Pickering pointed out, we "know what's what". The world of the Dallakers is huge, unknowable.

I used to hope that when the book was published Ned Kerne, wherever he is, would come forward and tell me the real ending of the story. But now I would be sorry if he did. Because when I lie awake at nights, I lie picturing for myself what might have happened on that wide beach that April daybreak. I strain into the salt, windy darkness for the lank, shadowy shapes of the Beachcombers, I listen for voices.

And I think this story will never have an ending for me, either.

THE NIGHT-WATCHMEN

Helen Cresswell

Josh and Caleb are no ordinary tramps. An air of mystery surrounds them, and Henry wants to know more.

He has so many questions: what does Josh mean when he calls himself a night-watchman? What is 'ticking'? And who are the menacing 'Greeneyes'?

Will Josh and Caleb ever trust Henry enough to let him in to their secret world – a world on the edge of reality. The final question is: where does the real world end, and fantasy begin?

ORDER FORM

0 340 73656 9 THE NIGHT-WATCHMEN £4.99 ❐
Helen Cresswell

All Hodder Children's books are available at your local bookshop, or can be ordered direct from the publisher. Just tick the titles you would like and complete the details below. Prices and availability are subject to change without prior notice.

Please enclose a cheque or postal order made payable to *Bookpoint Ltd*, and send to: Hodder Children's Books, 39 Milton Park, Abingdon, OXON OX14 4TD, UK.
Email Address: orders@bookpoint.co.uk

If you would prefer to pay by credit card, our call centre team would be delighted to take your order by telephone. Our direct line *01235 400414* (lines open 9.00 am–6.00 pm Monday to Saturday, 24 hour message answering service). Alternatively you can send a fax on *01235 400454*.

TITLE		FIRST NAME		SURNAME	

ADDRESS			
DAYTIME TEL:		POST CODE	

If you would prefer to pay by credit card, please complete:
Please debit my Visa/Access/Diner's Card/American Express (delete as applicable) card no:

Signature .... Expiry Date ....

If you would NOT like to receive further information on our products please tick the box. ❐